DANGEROUS HEART

By Tracey Bateman

DEFIANT HEART
DISTANT HEART

DANGEROUS HEART

Tracey Bateman

AVON

INSPIRE

An Imprint of HarperCollins*Publishers*

This is a work of fiction. Names, characters, places, and incidents are products of the author's imagination or are used fictitiously and are not to be construed as real. Any resemblance to actual events, locales, organizations, or persons, living or dead, is entirely coincidental.

HarperCollins books may be purchased for educational, business, or sales promotional use. For information please write: Special Markets Department, HarperCollins Publishers Inc., 10 East 53rd Street, New York, NY 10022.

FIRST EDITION

Interior text designed by Elizabeth M. Glover

Library of Congress Cataloging-in-Publication Data
  Bateman, Tracey Victoria.
    Dangerous heart / Tracey Bateman. — 1st ed.
      p.cm. — (Westward hearts)
    ISBN 978-0-06-124635-7
    I. Title.
PS3602.A854D36   2008
813'.6—dc22   2008016580

08 09 10 11 12   OV/RRD   10 9 8 7 6 5 4 3 2 1

For Ginger Nixon.
You have always been a mentor and friend.
There is not room enough for me to tell you how much I
love you. For twenty-four years God has used you to love
me, correct me, heal me, deliver me, and increase my faith
in Him. You serve God and His people with a singleness of
purpose and for His glory alone.
You make me want to know Him more.

One

Mid-October 1850

Gunfire in the middle of the night was never good.

The blast startled Ginger Freeman from the first sound sleep she'd had in a week. She bolted upright in the tent she shared with her friend and fellow traveler, Toni Rodden, and fumbled around in the dark for her moccasins.

"Was that thunder?" Toni asked from the other side of the tent, her voice thick with sleep and worry. She made a shadowy figure as she sat up and reached for her shoes.

"No. Gunfire. I'm going to check on it."

"You don't suppose it's Indians?" Toni's voice shook the words into the air.

Ginger understood her friend's fear. Only a short time ago, Toni had been the object of a young war chief's obsession. But the army had taken care of that—soon after Toni's rescue, a group of soldiers bore down upon the renegades' camp, rescuing white captives and rounding up as many of the braves as they could. "If it is a pack of

Indians, it's not who you're thinking. But you'd best stay put, just the same."

More gunfire shattered the night, and the sound of yelling echoed through the camp. "Outlaws! Take cover!"

"Did you hear that?" Toni asked, standing and heading toward the tent flap. "I—I better go with you."

The offer brought a smile to Ginger's lips. "I think we can handle it. Sam would have my hide if I let you go out there, and you know it. And I don't think it's outlaws, anyhow. Most likely Kip Caldwell and some of the other boys playing a joke with gunpowder and a flint." Ginger frowned, hard-pressed to believe her own words, but she tried to sound light-hearted for Toni's sake. "Besides, what kind of crazy outlaws would attack a wagon train the size of this one?"

"The kind with a lot of men and guns?" Toni's voice still shook, but Ginger had no time to mollycoddle her friend. She figured her help was most needed out there with the rest of the guns. More than the rest, truth be told. If there was one thing Ginger knew a little something about, it was outlaws—a fact she couldn't mention to Toni or anyone else. But from her experience, this attack just didn't make any kind of sense. Unless the bandits thought there was an awful lot of treasure to be had among this battered, weary band of travelers, or the men firing into the camp were missing a few brains. Ginger was betting on the latter.

"I'll be back as soon as I can." She checked to make sure her pistol was loaded, then stuffed it into her holster and grabbed her rifle for good measure. She tossed a quick look in Toni's direction. "Hunker down and stay out of sight. Hopefully this'll all be over soon."

"Be careful!" Toni whispered after her. Ginger stopped and turned back. She snatched her pistol from her holster. "Here, take this."

Toni gave a vehement shake of her head. "You'll need it. Besides, I don't like those things."

Ginger shoved the weapon toward her. Now was not the time to take no for an answer. "Take it. I have my rifle. How am I supposed to concentrate, thinking about you unprotected in here, all by yourself?"

Toni's expression softened, and she took the pistol. "Thank you, Ginger."

Ginger ducked her head, swallowing hard. Emotional women always made her uncomfortable. Maybe because she hadn't really spent much time in the company of women since she was a little girl. Before her ma left. She'd been raised around rough men, who laughed at tears and didn't cotton to hugs and coddling. "I'd best be going."

Pulling back the tent flap, she escaped outside, taking care to keep her head down and her senses alert. She gripped her rifle firmly, ready to aim and fire if necessary. And she figured it would be necessary real soon.

She tried to take stock of the situation. Outside the circle of wagons, the dark and dust and sagebrush were thick enough to hide a few outlaws, bent on mischief. But she still couldn't imagine anyone crazy enough to go up against a wagon train the size of this one. Especially if her suspicions were correct—no more than fifteen men would be riding with the outlaws.

She strained her eyes against the dimness around her. Dawn was beginning to break over the snow-capped mountains to the east, but it was still too dark to make out more than shadows beyond the camp's fires.

Ginger crept forward, bending at the waist as she tried to assess the situation. Her body remained tense, every inch of her alert to the danger lurking in the shadowy darkness, as she searched for the most logical spot to hunker down and make the biggest impact. From the direction of the gunfire, she knew they weren't surrounded, and the attack seemed to be aimed toward the middle of the wagon train.

Heading toward the closest wagon, she kept her mind focused on getting to her hiding spot—which was the only explanation for what happened next.

Strong fingers gripped her buckskin-clad arm and spun her around. Grant Kelley stood over her, concern drawing his eyebrows together. "Ginger, you should get back inside that tent before you get hurt."

His chest rose and fell, and heavy breath released from his lips as puffy clouds in the cold air. His expression bore down on her, warning her not to argue.

But Ginger wasn't one to take a warning from the likes of Grant Kelley or anyone else, for that matter. "My gun's as good as yours, so mind your own business."

The words left her sharply and probably came out too loud for the situation, but her pride had taken a hit by the way she'd let him sneak up on her like that. Besides, she could do without Grant touching her for any reason. She didn't like the way he made her insides go soft.

"You're too bullheaded for your own good." Grant pulled her to the ground with him as a bullet whizzed past her ear. Ducking behind the wagon wheel, he took aim in the direction the bullet had come and fired off two shots, then turned back to her. "Remember last time you joined a man's fight? You got an arrow through your leg."

Humiliation burned her cheeks at the unnecessary reminder that he had been the one to pull that arrow out and patch her up while she laid on the ground in a dead faint. She yanked her arm from his grip and white-knuckled her rifle. She took aim, sending a couple of rounds into the same area of darkness. "Well, I don't plan on getting shot."

"See that you don't." He fired again. And again. "I don't have time to keep patching you up!"

"No one asked you to!" Not to be outdone, Ginger raised her rifle toward the woods and squeezed the trigger again. In a beat, she heard leaves and twigs crackling. "Fall back!" came a voice of authority. Web? "Ames got hisself hit in the shoulder."

Ginger's stomach churned. She knew that voice. And she knew Ames. Her suspicion was correct. That was no random outlaw band. That was Web and the rest of the gang. And they had finally made good on their threat to come after her if she didn't return within three months.

She'd been gone four.

The outlaws continued firing while they retreated, but Ginger couldn't bring herself to shoot into the woods again.

Web might be a sorry excuse for a pa, but he was the only one she had. She couldn't take any chances on shooting him.

She fired again, purposely aiming high.

A grunt pushed through Grant's throat, and he sent her a fierce frown. "What are you doing?"

Glaring back, Ginger lifted her chin. "What do you mean? I'm doing the same thing you're doing. I'm shooting at out-laws."

"Not exactly." He set his rifle on the ground and unhol-stered his revolver. He fired off five rounds. "I'm aiming at the outlaws. You're shooting over their heads."

Caught. There was nothing to do but . . . well, lie a little bit. "They're running away. Where I come from, we don't shoot a man in the back."

"I do when they're outlaws," Grant said firmly, snatching the rifle from her hands. He shoved his pistol into his holster and jerked his head toward his rifle. "If you're not going to fire your own gun, at least load for me." He continued to fire, first her rifle and then his, while Ginger loaded and reloaded as fast as she could.

Within minutes the gunfire stopped, but Ginger's mind continue to spin. She doubted they'd be back. They must have figured out they were fighting a losing battle. Web was short of courage. He rarely entered a fight he didn't know he could win. That's why this was so odd.

Scowling, Grant shook his head. "You might as well have stayed in the tent with Toni, for all the help you were. What got into you?"

"I told you . . ."

"I know—you don't shoot folks in the back." He looked at her askance. "That didn't seem to bother you during the Indian attacks."

"That was different. Those varmints were after Toni."

"I'm not arguing with you." He reached down and offered her a hand up. Ginger glared and ignored it as she shoved up to her feet.

"Stubborn woman," Grant muttered, dropping his hand back to his side.

Ginger chose not to respond as slowly, cautiously, the members of the wagon train took courage from the silence and ventured out.

Grant bent and retrieved her rifle from the ground. "Here," he said.

All Ginger could muster was a grudging nod and a luke-warm, "Thanks."

"Listen, I'm sorry if I got a little rough back there." His lips slipped upwards into an apologetic smile. "But someone has to look out for you."

Ginger blinked and stared. If he'd yelled at her, called her names, even smacked her, she'd have no trouble holding her own. But this boyish grin mingled with soft, kind words—those things, hitting her all at once, disarmed her and left her mute. Just as she was about to recover her speech and tell him she could take care of herself, thank you very much, someone yelled from across the camp.

"Doc!"

She was glad for the opportunity to get away from the man she had spent the last seven years hating. A man who was slowly chipping away at her anger with every smile, every kind word, every unconscious touch.

"Sounds like someone's hurt." She averted her eyes, unwilling to find herself captured in his gaze. "You best get going."

"Hang on a second," he said. "If there are several injuries, I might need some help."

Panic welled in Ginger's chest. She couldn't help with gunshot wounds. Not after Clem. She still had nightmares about the blood on her hands after trying to stop her older brother's bleeding.

She would have bolted, but staring into Katie Caldwell's wide, fear-filled eyes, she couldn't move. "Doc!" The thirteen-year-old girl gulped the frigid morning air. "Miss Sadie says come quick. Yellow Bird's time has come and she's having a rough go of it."

"I'll be right there." Grant turned to Ginger and placed his big hands on her shoulders. "Go to the supply wagon and bring the black doctor's bag to Miss Sadie's tent. It's on the right when you go in. Please hurry. You know if Miss Sadie called for me, something must be wrong."

For once, Ginger didn't chafe against an order. She didn't argue. Nor did she speak. Instead, she nodded and took off at a run to do as she'd been instructed.

Grant entered Miss Sadie's tent without waiting to be invited. The woman had one of the few tents in camp that was large enough for a grown man to stand up straight. Most were sleeping tents and one had to stoop over to child height to get from the door to the pallet.

Yellow Bird writhed in pain on a pallet but didn't utter a sound. The young Sioux woman had joined the wagon train only recently. She'd come to them while running from a cruel fur trader who had bought her from her father under the pretense of marriage. His threats against her hadn't caused her flight, but when he revealed his intention to sell her baby to the Pawnees, she'd known she had no choice. The woman was a hero, as far as Grant was concerned. Surely someone with that much strength of character could deliver a baby, even under difficult circumstances. But Miss Sadie wouldn't have called him unless she couldn't help Yellow Bird on her own. That scared him.

Miss Sadie knelt beside the young woman and massaged her bulging belly. She had helped with the birthing of every baby born in the wagon train since they headed out from Independence nearly five months earlier, and Grant had no doubt that if the older woman was concerned, it was with good reason.

She stood when she saw him, her face drawn with worry, and took him by the arm. Pulling him back outside into the chill of the new dawn air, she said, "I didn't want Yellow Bird to hear."

"What's the trouble?"

The tension in her tone was thick, and she spoke with an uncommon lack of confidence. "I think the babe's stuck."

A chill ran up his spine. "How long has she been having pains?"

"Since yesterday afternoon."

Not too terribly long for a first baby, but he respected Miss Sadie's abilities and more importantly her opinions when it came to birthing babies. "I'll have to take a look at her to confirm it."

"The sooner the better," Miss Sadie said. "I'm afraid we're going to lose them both if something isn't done."

Returning inside, Grant knelt at the end of Yellow Bird's pallet and examined her. Miss Sadie's assessment was correct. The baby was stuck in the birth canal, his shoulder caught and unable to dislodge to finish the birthing process.

He nodded to Miss Sadie. "You're right. The baby is stuck," he said grimly. "I need to pray."

He took Yellow Bird's hand. She stared up at him, eyes filled with pain and fear. "My baby?"

"We need to get him out soon, or he'll die." Grant reached forward and smoothed a strand of silky black hair from her forehead. "Do you know Jesus?"

Yellow Bird nodded.

"Okay, then we're going to pray that God will help me deliver your baby safely."

He kept her hand firmly inside of his, and they closed their eyes just as Ginger barreled in. "I brought the bag." She stopped short, her chest heaving as she fought for breath. "What's going on? Why are your eyes closed?"

Grant looked up and caught her wild-eyed gaze. She handed him the black bag. "How is she?" She looked down at Yellow Bird without awaiting an answer. "You okay?"

The Indian woman nodded, pain dulling her eyes and causing her breath to come in soft bursts between her words. "The baby is not coming as he should. We must pray now."

"That's why our eyes were closed," Miss Sadie said, her expression filled with admonishment for the brash young woman.

"Okay." Ginger's face was void of all color, and it was easy to see the worry in her eyes. She shifted as an awkward silence consumed time they didn't have. "I'll just wait outside until you're done."

"Kneel down, Ginger," Grant said firmly. "Close your eyes and be quiet while we pray."

Yellow Bird nodded, her teary eyes filled with pleading as she looked up at Ginger. "You pray too. For my baby."

Ginger's face gentled, touching a place in Grant's heart. Something about the way she loved her friends spoke to Grant. He'd seen it before. Loyalty ran fiercely through her blood. Despite her obvious desire to run away, she knelt beside Yellow Bird and took the woman's trembling hand.

Then she opened her mouth. "Okay, but God hasn't ever answered any of my prayers before," she muttered. "I don't see why He'd start now."

Grant looked at Yellow Bird, then back at Ginger, and cleared his throat softly. Ginger nodded a little as though she understood his meaning and brightened marginally. "This is probably my lucky day, though," she hastily—and poorly, in Grant's opinion—tried to amend.

"Grant, there isn't a lot of time," Miss Sadie urged.

With a nod, Grant closed his eyes. "Let's pray." They

bowed their heads and he began to speak. "Lord, give me wisdom and mercy to bring this baby safely into Your beautiful world. Show me how to dislodge this child and bring it forth. Amen."

Ginger gave a tug on Grant's shirt. "I have an idea that might work."

"What is it?" he asked, barely listening.

"I once saw a farmer trying to help out this old cow."

"Ginger, please," Miss Sadie said with weary annoyance. "Just hush. Your storytelling isn't helping Yellow Bird."

"It might, if you two would just listen to me." Ginger's voice held her own frustration. Grant glanced at her and met her gaze. Fear grazed her brown eyes, and he felt himself responding to her need to be heard.

"All right," he said, "but hurry up."

"The cow was having a rough go of it, and Mr. Murdock reached in and turned the calf, gave it a yank, and it came out."

Grant rubbed Yellow Bird's rock-hard belly, hoping the baby would dislodge itself from wherever it seemed to be hung up. "Well, a calf isn't a baby."

"I know that," Ginger said, scowling. "Don't you think I know the difference?"

"I'm sure you do and I know you want to help, but right now, I need to concentrate."

Yellow Bird shifted on the pallet. Sweat glistened on her neck and forehead. Grant knew she had to be in excruciating pain, still she barely made a sound.

Ginger, on the other hand, couldn't seem to keep quiet.

"Why can't you just hear me out? That calf was good as dead, and Mr. Murdock saved it."

"Please, Ginger! I'm doing my best." All the fire left Ginger's eyes, and she nodded quickly, stepping back to give him room to move.

The thought of reaching inside the Indian woman and turning the child scared him. Terrified him, in fact. He caught Miss Sadie's gaze. Dark circles surrounded her eyes and the lines on her face seemed more pronounced than he'd ever noticed. "You know, as unlikely as it seems, you might give Ginger's suggestion a try, Grant," she said. "I've seen it work before."

Still, Grant hesitated. How could he bear it if the child died in his hands, along with Yellow Bird? "It's risky."

"But not impossible," she countered. "And at least it's better than sitting here doing nothing, while Yellow Bird and her baby die."

Grant's stomach churned at the image. "You're right. It's not impossible. With God, all things are possible."

But his thoughts flashed to another young mother he couldn't save. The memory caused his hands to tremble. Of course, his wife, Sarah, had only been in her third month of pregnancy, and her death wasn't related to her condition. Still, Yellow Bird's situation brought back all of his fears and insecurities. His inability to save the love of his life had been the reason he stopped practicing medicine in the first place.

Struggling against a desire to walk out of the tent and turn his back completely on the entire wagon train, he forced himself to study the pain on Yellow Bird's face. He had to be strong and do his best. Otherwise, it wouldn't be God that failed; it would be him.

"Yellow Bird," he said softly, caressing her sweat-soaked brow. "Your baby is not able to come any further because he isn't in the right position. I am going to try to turn him and pull him out. It will be painful, and there are no guarantees. But we have to try. Do you understand?"

She nodded, and another contraction rocked her small body. "If you do nothing, my child will not live."

"That's right." He made no mention that she would likely die, as well. But he figured she knew, and there was something to be said for keeping hope alive.

Yellow Bird gripped his hand and lifted her shoulders off the pallet. She gave him a hard, pleading stare. "Please, doctor. You must try."

Grant sprang into action. The young woman was growing weaker by the minute. "Ginger, Miss Sadie, get on either side of Yellow Bird and don't let her thrash about too much."

"Me?" Ginger's voice sounded faint. "I'll go get Toni or Fannie. I'll be right back."

"There's no time!" Grant grabbed the white-faced girl by the shoulders and gave her a little shake. "Ginger! You have to be strong. I know you don't like illness or blood. But you can*not* faint, is that clear?"

"Who said I was going to faint?"

Good! Some of her spunk was showing.

Grant tried to ignore the sound of Yellow Bird's groans as he felt for the baby's head, and then the shoulder.

He looked up at Miss Sadie. "Hold her."

Slowly he tried to turn the baby. Still, with the next pain, the baby didn't descend any farther. "I have to try to turn him the other way," he said more to himself than the women. He could hear his panic. "Lord, please," he whispered.

"Pray, Ladies."

Ginger prayed the same two words over and over like a mantra. "Please God, please God, please God, please God—" Finally Grant's nerves could take it no longer.

"Ginger! Stop!"

"Well, you're the one that told me to pray!"

"Can't you pray something else?"

Yellow Bird let out a scream of pain that pierced the interior of the tent.

"It's the only prayer I know!" Ginger resumed her petition. "Please God, please God, please God, please God."

As Grant turned the infant counterclockwise, he felt the shoulder begin to dislodge. Hope sprang up inside his heart, and he found himself joining in Ginger's prayer. "Please God, please God, please God."

Moments later, a healthy boy slid into the world with lusty cries that brought a slow, exhausted smile to his mother's pale lips.

"Would you look at that?" Ginger said, excitement and wonder in her tone. Miss Sadie wrapped the baby and tried to give him to Yellow Bird. The young woman had fainted. "Ginger, take the baby," Miss Sadie said. "I need to help Grant take care of Yellow Bird. She's bleeding too heavily."

"I don't know if I can," Ginger said, the fear in her voice so thick Grant could almost reach out and touch it.

"It's okay," Miss Sadie said with uncommon gentleness that surprised Grant. "There's nothing to it. You'll do just fine."

Miss Sadie slipped the baby carefully into Ginger's arms. A soft gasp caused Grant to raise his head just for a second. His stomach jumped at the sight of the young woman holding Yellow Bird's baby. Ginger's lips parted slightly, and her eyes widened as she looked from the infant to him.

He would have never thought this possible. For all of her spit and fire and annoying behavior, Ginger Freeman could be as soft as any woman when holding a baby.

Later, as he went about his daily rounds, he couldn't escape the image of her eyes, moist and filled with wonder, and her lips, soft and slightly parted, as she stared at the miracle in her arms.

Two

Ginger's back ached from sitting next to Yellow Bird on the hard ground all day. Grant had warned that the Indian woman was still bleeding a little more heavily than he liked and should not be left alone. And that was fine with Ginger. She wouldn't have been able to concentrate on anything else today anyway.

On the pallet in the corner of the tent, Miss Sadie stirred from a nap and sat up. A yawn and a stretch later, she shook her head. "I must have dozed off. It's been a long night." A frown creased her brow. "What are you still doing here, Ginger?"

"Grant said we should keep an eye on these two."

Miss Sadie let out an exasperated breath. "I don't think he meant literally sit next to her and stare at her while she sleeps. Why don't you go make yourself useful somewhere instead of hovering? Mercy's sake, if she wakes up sudden-like, you'll scare her to death."

The sting of Miss Sadie's words cut Ginger to the core. How could the old widow have the gall to suggest that she wasn't being useful? Hadn't she brought the doctor's bag and stayed when they prayed and let Yellow Bird grip her hand until she was almost sure the tiny woman was going to squeeze her fingers right off? And hadn't she been the one to suggest turning the baby? Grant had even thanked her, and Miss Sadie herself admitted that God had spoken through Ginger. If the Almighty had thought her special enough to voice His wisdom through, then maybe Miss Sadie ought to start showing her a little bit of respect.

Now that it was all over, she'd dedicated herself to watching over the new mother and her tiny babe so Miss Sadie could take a nap. The implication that she was in the way just galled Ginger more than she could say. Ungrateful old woman!

She jerked her chin and folded her arms across her chest. "I'm not going anywhere until Doc says Yellow Bird is out of the woods."

"Trust me. I've delivered enough babies to know that she's come through the worst of it. Yellow Bird and Little Sam are both going to be fine." Miss Sadie muscled her way around Ginger and placed her hand on Yellow Bird's forehead. She gave a satisfied nod. "No fever, praise the Lord."

Relief poured over Ginger, and her mind echoed the praise heavenward, though she'd rather die than admit it. "Well, that's good. Right? No infection?" Even though Yellow Bird had lost more blood than she should have and was therefore weaker than most new mothers, Grant had assured her that as long as no infection set in, Yellow Bird should make a full recovery.

"Look, Ginger, honey," Miss Sadie said, her tone conciliatory. She obviously realized the bullying approach hadn't worked. Now she was being nice. Too nice. And Ginger wasn't a bit fooled. She stayed planted on the ground with her arms folded. "I said I'm not moving until Yellow Bird wakes up."

"I'm awake." The soft sound of Yellow Bird's voice barely penetrated the tent.

Ginger's protective nature took over. "You shouldn't be, Yellow Bird. Doc says you need your rest."

Miss Sadie let out a huff. "How could she not be, with all your yammering?"

Ginger ignored her and kept her attention on her friend. Fever or no fever, as far as Ginger was concerned, the pale face was cause for worry.

"You feelin' okay?"

Yellow Bird gave a weary nod. "I am fine." She looked lovingly at the tiny creature lying in the crook of her arm. "Is he not beautiful? My heart sings a new song." The baby stirred at the sound of his mother's voice and let out a faint mewing noise.

Ginger's heart lurched. "Is he okay?"

Yellow Bird's lips curved into a smile. "He is hungry." She adjusted and pulled at a leather thong at her shoulder, loosening the top of her buckskin dress.

Ginger's face heated as the baby latched on and began nursing with greedy, sucking noises.

She cleared her throat and rose to her feet. "I have things to do."

"About time," Miss Sadie muttered.

"I'll be back later, Yellow Bird." Without awaiting a response, Ginger opened the flap and stepped outside into the chilly autumn twilight.

Blake Tanner, the wagon master had called a halt for one day in the aftermath of this morning's attack, followed by the birth of Yellow Bird's baby. A baby's birth wouldn't normally be grounds for losing a day of travel, especially when the group was already a month behind schedule, but Ginger had overheard Grant telling Miss Sadie that Yellow Bird might not live through a hard day of traversing the deep wagon ruts in the worn trail ahead.

The concern in Grant's voice had sent a wave of fear through Ginger. She'd never had a real female friend except for Toni Rodden, but Yellow Bird had earned Ginger's respect when she'd helped save Toni from being kidnapped and sold to a Cheyenne war chief. Was it any wonder she had ignored Miss Sadie's annoyance and refused to budge from Yellow Bird's side while her life was in danger?

Filled with excess energy, Ginger headed for her horse, Tulip. She knew from experience that the only way to release her frustration and relax was to ride at breakneck speed until she felt herself calm down. Tulip released a breath in anticipation as Ginger cinched the saddle tight and climbed on the mare's back. Besides, after the Almighty had been so good as to answer her prayer about Yellow Bird, she figured she owed Him a little bit of conversation.

"Ginger!" Grant Kelley stormed toward her. "Where do you think you're going?"

Ginger's stomach tightened at his tone. He would be telling her she couldn't go. Well, she wouldn't stand for it. "For a ride. Not that it's any of your concern."

"Didn't you hear Blake's orders that no one is to ride off alone today?" His eyes blazed.

Ginger sent him a fierce scowl. "I didn't hear any such thing."

"Well, he said it. Besides, after this morning's attack, you shouldn't have to be told. It's almost dark. You wouldn't get a mile from here without night setting in. Use your head."

"I always use my head." And she resented the implication that she wasn't. "The moon and stars are bright. I'll find my way just fine." Ginger jerked her horse around. After all, she had ridden on her own for two months before joining up with the wagon train. And evaded detection from Grant and his scouts during that time. She could take care of herself.

"You aren't going anywhere, you stubborn woman. Blake's orders. Besides, you know what he said last time you rode off without permission. Do you want to take a chance on forcing his hand?"

Ginger shifted uncomfortably in her saddle. She did remember. Blake had irrevocably announced he'd leave her behind at the next fort if she disobeyed orders again. In this case, the fort in question was Fort Boise, and they'd be there in a few short days. She had no intention of being left behind. Still, how could she stay cooped up inside camp when the wide open beckoned after such a long and difficult day?

Besides, she hadn't heard Blake say anything about folks staying in camp and not riding off alone. And she wouldn't even consider the likely possibility that he actually had given that order. Admitting the possibility meant she had better stay put. Glancing across the plain, she hesitated, but only long enough to make a firm decision.

A gentle nudge to Tulip's flank was all it took for the mare to bolt and run, leaving Grant in a cloud of dust, his face mottled in anger. Ginger grinned as she put distance between herself and the wagon train. Even if Grant saddled up and rode hard, he'd never catch her. She didn't care a bit. Let him be mad. Grant was a bully and always tried to tell her what to do. He might not remember her. After all she had been only eleven years old when they'd last met. But she remembered him well, and he would soon find out that she had her own bone to pick with the doc. The folks of this wagon train would discover that Grant Kelley wasn't everything he pretended to be.

After a few minutes, her head began to clear. She looked up into the gathering darkness and figured now was as good a time as any to have that conversation with the Almighty.

She cleared her throat. "Uh . . ." This was strange. How did Toni and Fannie and Blake and just about everyone she knew just talk into air without thinking anything of it? "You know I'm not much of one to talk out loud to a person that probably isn't even there. But just in case . . . I'd like to thank You for bringing Yellow Bird's babe and keeping them both alive."

That was about all she could muster. And even at that, her face was as hot as July at the very thought that someone might have heard.

She began to regret her hasty actions in riding off. What if Blake really had ordered everyone to stay in camp? It sounded like something the conscientious wagon master would say. If he got wind of her disobedience, it might be the final straw for him. Not that Ginger deliberately got herself into trouble, but it just seemed to find her when she least expected it. She slowed Tulip to a trot and finally to a walk. "I think I might have messed up again, girl," she said, leaning forward and throwing her arms about Tulip's neck. "But Grant is like a burr in my saddle. And I know you know what that's like. Why can't he stop acting all high-and-mighty all the time?"

If only he knew why she'd joined the wagon train in the first place, he'd be a lot more careful how he treated her. That was for certain.

Why hadn't she done what she had come to do? For seven years, all she had wanted was the satisfaction of seeing Grant pay. It had taken her that long to convince Web to let her do it, too. So why, after more than two months of traveling with the wagon train, hadn't she?

These folks on the wagon train . . . they were different from the band of thieves and thugs she'd grown up with. The thought of doing what she'd come to do and returning to the band of outlaws waiting for her return didn't sit right. As a matter of fact, it filled her nightmares. The only explanation was that all this talk about God had somehow sunk in more than she'd ever thought possible.

As the child of a prostitute and an outlaw, Ginger had never heard about Jesus until arriving on the wagon train. God was simply a curse word, except her ma used to cry and pray to Him when she was drunk. It hadn't occurred to Ginger that the life they led was wrong. Gambling, drinking, and outlawing. That was her world until a few months ago. Life in the train had changed her. And not just on the inside, either. She'd started taking regular baths. Toni had forced her to initially, but now she actually enjoyed being clean. She attended when Sam Two Feathers preached, and she was even starting to understand and look forward to the meetings. God was becoming real instead of myth, and prayer seemed more than drunken petitions. Going back to her former life filled her with dread. And not only dread, but out-and-out fear. Given the choice, she wouldn't return.

But if she didn't get herself back to camp before Blake figured out she'd disobeyed his orders, she'd be on her own and might not have any choice.

With a sigh, she sat up, patting Tulip's neck. She noted the wagon train was so far in the distance, she could barely see the smoke rising from the campfires and the circled wagons.

"Dadburn it," she muttered. "I didn't know we went that far." With a kick to Tulip's flanks, she headed back toward the wagon train. But just as the mare broke into a trot, the sound of horses coming from behind shot fear up her spine. She spun around in the saddle, finding herself surrounded by a dozen or more riders. Her heart slammed against her chest as she gripped her rifle without lifting it from the holder on her saddle. No one had to tell her who they were, even before her eyes adjusted to the waning light. "So it *was* you," she said to the group in general. Gratified that her voice barely shook, she made an even sweep of the motley bunch. Laughter rumbled through the band of outlaws. "That's right, gal." Her pa rode forward.

"What are you doing so far from home, Web?" she asked.

"Well, whaddaya think we're doin'? We come lookin' for you," Web said.

"Yeah," a shadowy figure spoke up. Ginger recognized his voice—that sarcastic, haughty voice, setting her teeth on edge. "Besides there's too blasted many wanted posters in Kansas and Missouri for us to stay put. We thought we'd follow your trail and see if you're ready to come back. We got a new job planned."

"Shut up, Lane," Web commanded. "No one asked you to talk for me."

Faced with the reality of Web's presence, a sudden fear dropped over Ginger like a heavy robe. She wasn't the same person they had known. How could she explain how she had changed, without causing Web to force her to leave the wagon train?

"Well?" Web growled. He gave a shudder and hunched over from the waist.

"You okay, Web?"

"Don't worry about me, gal." The look on his face was so fierce, Ginger shrank back. She must have imagined his moment of weakness.

"S-sorry, Web."

"Forget sorry," he snapped. "Just answer the question."

"What question?"

Web's eyes narrowed. "You sassin' me, gal?"

Swallowing hard, she shook her head as the memory of his backhand against her cheek made her cower. "No. But I didn't hear the question."

"That's because there wasn't one spoken."

Ginger's heart did a flip as the moonlight illuminated the chiseled features of a man she'd never seen before. A square jaw, wide-set eyes, a firm brow. He wore a leather coat and a bandana around his neck.

"Mind yer own business, Elijah," Web said.

Was that sweat on his forehead? Ginger frowned. How could he be sweating in this cold? Forcing her gaze and concern away from Web, she settled on the newcomer. "My apologies." His gaze never left Ginger. He smiled when he spoke. "I believe Web would like to know if you're ready to return to the fold."

"She knows what I mean." Web stared down the newcomer, but clearly was losing the battle of wills. He turned his attention back to Ginger, giving her a squinty-eyed glare. "Now, I've given you plenty of time. It's time to come back, whether you got it done or not."

Web's aversion to revenge was the reason he'd taken so long to allow her to go after Grant in the first place. He considered it a waste of energy.

"It's not that simple, Web. I can't just walk up to him and put a gun to his head."

"Don't believe her, Web. She's done gone soft. I can see it, plain as day." Lane Conners had been riding with Web for so long Web treated him like a son. But that didn't mean Ginger was going to take any nonsense from him.

Ginger bristled under his teasing grin. But she refused to engage in a useless argument with a useless man.

Web shifted in his saddle. He glared at Lane. "Leave her alone."

Lane leaned forward, his movement mimicking Web's. The way his eyes raked over her caused all the hair on Ginger's neck to stand up straight. He didn't have to say a word for her to hear him loudly. She never felt quite right around Lane. Even if Web believed him to be the one to take over for him some day.

Web turned a silent gaze on her and frowned. "What are you sayin'?"

Ginger jerked her chin and held herself straight in the saddle. "I'm trying to take care of it without getting a wanted poster with my face on it. Sometimes you got to be smart about things."

All humor fled Lane's face. "You sayin' we men ain't as smart as you?"

"Would she be wrong?"

Once again the newcomer was speaking up on her behalf. Ginger's heart lifted at the support. Lane, on the other hand, didn't seem nearly as impressed.

Lane turned. "Shut up, Elijah. You don't even know her."

"Ah, you do make a striking point. Perhaps I've been presumptuous." He sent Ginger a wink. She couldn't help but be amused by his baiting.

Lane gave a satisfied nod, but Elijah added with a half-grin, "I do, however, know you. And I can't argue with her implication."

Without awaiting a response from Lane, he urged his horse forward and tipped his hat to Ginger. "As Lane so astutely pointed out, I haven't had the pleasure of your acquaintance, Miss Freeman."

Web moved his horse forward. Ginger tensed. Web had already told Elijah to mind his own business. He wouldn't stand for the man's interference for too awful long. No telling what was about to happen, but one thing was sure—it wouldn't end nicely for Elijah. "This is my girl, Ginger. Ginger, this is Elijah Garrett. Started riding with us directly after you run off."

Ginger bristled. It wasn't like she'd run away. She had a mission to accomplish—a seven-year-old mission. One that she'd finally felt ready to undertake after she'd spotted Grant among the travelers in Hawkins, Kansas. It was a stroke of luck that the gang had ridden into that rough prairie town the day before the train arrived. After all that time of reliving the day her older brother had died—all that time hating the doctor with a fiery passion—she'd been given a gift. The chance to make him pay. There wasn't much law in Hawkins, so the gang camped out in the area and rode into town when restlessness got the better of them and they wanted to visit the local saloons. Grant Kelley had been at the general store, looking at oil for rubbing on leather, when she'd spotted him. Hightailing it back to camp, she shook with excitement as she told the rest of the gang whom she'd just seen.

Web thought it was foolishness but had given in—as long as she returned in three months. At first, she'd simply trailed the wagon train, keeping back a safe distance and eating jerky meat day in and day out, rather than risk a fire. If there was one thing Web had taught her, it was how to hide. To lay in wait and not get herself caught. So that's what she'd done, as she waited for a chance to catch Grant alone.

That time had finally come when the wagon train halted outside of Fort Laramie. Most of the settlers had gone to the fort, but the doctor hadn't. With so few guards remaining in camp, the timing seemed perfect. Another gift. But Toni's scream had shattered the silence that night as Ginger followed him and when she ran to the other woman's assistance, she'd been discovered. A couple of days later, Sam Two Feathers, the head scout for the train, had offered her a job, keeping an eye on Toni Rodden. Since then, she'd made herself a valuable member of the wagon train through her tracking and hunting abilities.

Why did Web have to show up out of nowhere and ruin it all?

The stranger cleared his throat rather loudly and she realized that he was waiting for an acknowledgement from her. "Nice to meet you Elijah."

"Likewise."

She turned to her pa. "He's the only doctor on the wagon train. If I kill him now, it might be bad for the rest of the folks." Web shook his head. And again, Ginger noted the way he hunched over at the waist.

"You sure you're okay, Web? You seem awfully sick to me."

"You let me worry about me. Let's talk about you. It's time, gal. You either do what you came to do, or you give up the notion. Either way, you been gone long enough. We got to get on with things."

Lane released a quick breath. "We got to get on with the new plan, and we need her to do it. I say, we let the doctor go, and Ginger comes back to the gang."

Web pierced him with a look so fierce, even Ginger shrank from it. "Since when did you start givin' orders around here?"

Lane retreated. "Sorry, Web. Just makin' a suggestion."

"Well, don't," Web snapped. He slanted a gaze at Ginger, his expression leaving no doubt in her mind that he was serious. "You got a week. Then it's time to come back to us. We got a plan, and we need a female to pull it off."

Ginger swallowed hard. "What do you mean? What kind of plan? I thought I was done with helping out that way."

"You was, but you ain't a young'un no more. It's time you started earnin' your keep."

She didn't have the nerve to say what she wanted to say— that she'd just as soon they leave without her. That she'd rather make her own way than have to go back to the outlaw band. That she'd finally learned what it was to associate with decent, hard-working folks who valued her for what she offered as a person. "Look, Web, I have to go. They're going to expect me back pretty soon."

Lane let out a snort. "They're expecting you back? You answer to those people now?"

"I have to fit in, or they'll get suspicious."

"The little lady's right," Elijah spoke up with a silky smooth voice that in no way matched his profession, as far as Ginger was concerned. "There's a smart way and a foolish way to go about these things. She's chosen the smart approach. Patience shows intelligence." He smiled a lazy smile. "And virtue."

Web let out a grunt and stared the new member of the gang to silence, then turned back to Ginger. "You go on back. But remember what I said. One week. Oh, and keep an eye out for Buddy. He never came back with us after the raid this morning."

"Buddy? I thought he was going to study with that doctor in Hawkins."

"Dr. Michaels?" Web spat as though the very word tasted foul. "Turns out he weren't really a doctor. Couldn't even set a broken leg. Too bad, too. We coulda used a doctor around here." He grunted and touched his hand to his side and winced.

"You suffering?" Ginger asked, then cringed as she waited for his bark.

"I told you I'm fine."

"Sorry, Web."

Poor Buddy. All he'd ever wanted was to study medicine. It would have been his chance for freedom—no matter what Web had planned. Buddy would have left and never come back. He wasn't cut out for being an outlaw any more than she was. Her fifteen-year-old brother was, by far, the youngest member of their group, and Ginger had hoped this opportunity would allow him a way out; otherwise, she never would have left him. "Web, how is it that no one noticed that he was gone before you got back to camp? He's just a boy."

"He's half-grown. The boy can take care of hisself." Web focused his gaze on her. "Besides, he'll likely be comin' to find you before he shows up back here."

Ginger hoped so. The alternative would mean he'd been shot during the raid and lay somewhere all alone, either dead or hurt.

She started to turn Tulip around then hesitated. "Listen, Web. Be careful and stay out of sight. The train has a couple of real sharp trackers. You won't be able to hide if you stay this close to the wagons."

He gave her a nod, and his expression seemed to soften a little in the moonlight. But that sickly look remained, touching off another round of worry in Ginger

"Ain't that touchin'? Don't listen to her, Web." Lane shifted in his saddle. "I think it's 'cause she knows there's something valuable in that wagon, and she wants it for herself. Why else would she have been gone this long?"

Her stomach dropped. Lane could only be referring to the supply wagon. It did have valuables in it, but mostly seed and supplies. Valuable to be sure—to a band of pioneers looking to build life and break land in a new country. Certainly nothing worth stealing for these thugs.

Web turned back to Ginger. "You get on back and keep your eyes and ears open for Buddy."

Ginger shrank back a little under his stern command. "Okay, Web."

She headed Tulip toward the camp, the quiver in her gut making her want to turn away, ride across the mountains, and never lay eyes on Web and his gang or the wagon train ever again.

Grant tried hard not to keep his gaze focused toward the west. He had plenty to do without worrying about a rough-talking, buckskin-wearing female. He expelled a frustrated breath. It was no use. He was worthless until he knew she was safe.

He slapped his thigh as the frustration hit him full in the

gut. She ought to be back by now. During the past fifteen minutes, clouds had begun to roll in, swallowing the light of the moon and stars, and it was near impossible to see past the glow of their own campfires.

He clomped awkwardly through camp, toward the direction she'd ridden.

"Good evening, Grant. What on earth could be plaguing your mind so much that you'd walk right by me without so much as a word of greeting?"

From her fire, Toni Rodden's amused voice transcended Grant's thoughts. He felt his ears warm as he changed his course and walked the five short steps to join her. "Sorry, Miss Toni," he muttered.

"Don't worry yourself about it. I was only teasing. Coffee?" Toni held up the tin pot. With a modest, crocheted shawl draped across her shoulders and her hair pinned up in a proper style, it was impossible to tell Toni had once been a fancy woman. For all intents and purposes, she looked just like the rest of the women in the wagon train. Only she was different. Special, in fact, because she'd caught the eye and captured the heart of Sam Two Feathers.

He glanced about, despite the futility of the action. "You haven't seen Ginger, have you?"

"Ginger? I assume she stayed with Yellow Bird all day. I haven't seen her since she hightailed it out of our tent during the outlaw raid this morning. Haven't you been over there to check on your patient?"

"Yes, I have. She isn't there."

"I'm sorry, then; I don't know where she is. Perhaps with Fannie?"

That did it. Grant expelled a frustrated breath. "I best go after her."

In the light of the fire, Toni's soft brow wrinkled in concern. "What do you mean?"

He glanced at the road west.

A soft gasp escaped her throat. "Do you mean to tell me Ginger rode off alone?"

"'Fraid so."

"But Blake ordered everyone to stay in camp. I heard him. Why on earth would Ginger do that? Especially after Blake warned her about disobeying orders."

"Why ask me anything about that woman? I don't understand why she does half of the things she does. She probably doesn't even know."

A smile tipped Toni's lips. "You may be right about that." She looked over his shoulder and gave a nod. "At any rate, you don't need to worry anymore. She's back."

Grant's stomach tightened with a combination of relief and irritation. He turned to find Ginger stomping back into camp leading Tulip—a ridiculous name for a horse, as far as Grant was concerned.

"Excuse me," he said to Toni, not bothering to remove his gaze from Ginger.

"Of course."

Grant's heart raced as he stalked the twenty yards across camp. Breathless, he reached Ginger just as she finished hobbling Tulip and turning her loose for the night.

"Where have you been?" he demanded.

She brushed past him, walking toward her tent. "Riding. Just like I told you earlier when I left."

"Don't you have any idea what might have happened out there?"

"'Evenin', Toni," she said, ignoring his words altogether.

Toni smiled. "I'm glad you're back safely."

Drawing herself up with attempted dignity, Ginger squared her shoulders. "Why wouldn't I be?"

Frustration beat a steady rhythm through his temples. "Ginger!"

"Land's sake!" She stomped one leg and jutted her chin. "Why won't you leave me alone?"

"Because I worry about you. You don't seem to understand that there are very real dangers out there, just waiting for a lone woman without a lot of fear and even less sense. Between outlaws, Indians, and wild animals, you're mighty lucky you weren't killed. I expected to find you dead."

A frown creased her brow and she looked toward Toni. "Can you please explain to Mr. Kelley that I'm not his responsibility and that I'd appreciate it if he'd just mind his own cockeyed business?"

Toni cleared her throat. "I would, except that he has a point. It was a little frightening, considering the circumstances, Ginger. If those outlaws are still out there—"

"Exactly," Grant burst in. "What if you'd run into those outlaws? Or a bear?"

Rolling her eyes, Ginger shook her head, twisting her face into a scowl directed solely at him. "I'm here aren't I?" she said with a huff he had grown accustomed to over the past couple of months. He didn't care for it any more now than the first time she'd directed her disdain in his direction. "Not that it's your business."

"It's my business when you disobey direct orders from the wagon master and put yourself in harm's way."

Her eyes shifted with fear. "What makes you think I was in harm's way?" She gulped.

Toni stepped forward. "Ginger, I think you should go find Blake and try to smooth this over. He's probably not thinking too highly of you right now. The best thing you could do is go to him before he sends for you."

Grant watched Ginger's face as her emotions clearly warred inside her. Finally, she gave a slow nod. "I reckon you're right."

Toni patted Ginger's shoulder. "I'll warm up some left over beans and a wedge of cornbread for when you get back."

Ginger rolled her eyes. "Don't bother. I doubt I'll be able to eat anything."

"Well, I'll warm it up just the same. Maybe Blake won't be too hard on you."

"Don't bet on it."

Grant watched her go, her feet shuffling along the rocky ground as she made her way to the wagon master's fire.

"Well," Toni said, "I know what I'm going to be doing for the next hour or so."

Grant turned to her. "What's that?"

A smile tipped her lips. "Praying for mercy."

"She's going to need it."

"Grant!" The sound of Sam Two Feathers's voice interrupted their conversation.

Toni's face brightened at the sight of her fiancé. "Good evening, Sam," she said. "Can I get you some coffee?"

Sam shook his head. "Nothing would give me more pleasure, but for now I must speak with Grant."

Toni's eyes showed only the briefest disappointment. She gave a nod. "All right. I'll see you later, then."

"I will stop by to say good night if your campfire is still burning when my duties are completed."

"I'll look forward to it."

Sam inclined his head away from Toni's camp, and Grant followed in the direction he indicated.

"Think Blake will force Ginger out at Fort Boise?"

The half-Sioux scout gave a shrug. "I have stopped trying to predict Blake's actions." He frowned. "But Ginger disobeys often. She must, at least, be punished, or the men of the wagon train will lose their desire to follow Blake the rest of the way to Oregon. They will not respect him."

That was an understatement if Grant had ever heard one. Ginger didn't understand the meaning of the word obedience. Well, she did, as long as that submission suited her immediate purposes. She certainly chose her moments to do as she was told.

"What is it you wanted to talk to me about, Sam?"

"Come with me," Sam said. "Blake is waiting for us in the supply tent."

"He is? Ginger just went to find him. She's hoping to worm her way out of trouble."

"Whether this is possible or not is up to Blake, but regardless, she will not find him for now. We will."

Grant knew better than to question the scout. If Two Feathers wanted to reveal the reason for this meeting, he would. Otherwise, Grant had no choice but to quell his curiosity and follow.

Three

Ginger's footsteps slowed with the dread of anticipation as she approached the wagon master's campsite. Fannie stood over a tub of dishwater, quietly singing to herself. Ginger's breathing increased as she gave a tentative glance about, preparing to face whatever fate Blake had in store for her.

Fannie flashed a broad smile as she glanced up and spotted her standing there. "Hi, Ginger." She pushed aside an errant curl from her forehead, then plunged her arms, up to her elbows, back into the sudsy water.

"Evenin', Fannie. Blake around?"

Fannie shook her red, curly head and blew upward at the curl that just wouldn't stay put. "He went to meet Sam."

"Oh, well, I suppose I'll have to wait, then."

Fannie nodded and grinned, the freckles on her scrunched up nose making her look much too young to be the wife of the most important man in the wagon train. "Camp business came up. He seemed as relieved to put off talking to you as you do."

In that smile, Ginger felt she had an ally. Her tension began to ease up.

On the other hand, if Fannie knew she needed an ally to begin with, then Ginger must really be in trouble.

Fannie grabbed a towel and dried her hands. "Want to wait? He shouldn't be long."

"I don't know . . ." Ginger's stomach let out a loud grumble reminding her that she hadn't eaten a morsel since supper the night before. She eyed the half-eaten rabbit still hanging over the fire. The sizzling meat looked a lot more appealing than the thought of beans and cornbread back at her own fire. Fannie's gaze followed hers. She gave a nod. "You want some? We've had our fill. I was planning to give the leftovers to Wolfie, but he can get his own, if you're hungry."

As much as she sympathized with the dog, the aroma of roasted rabbit played havoc with Ginger's empty stomach. She gave Fannie a grateful little nod. "I'd be obliged."

Fannie tossed the towel across the edge of the tub and headed toward the fire with a tin plate. "Have a seat, then. I'll dish it up."

Ginger took her place on the pickle barrel Fannie had indicated. In spite of herself, she heaved a great sigh.

Fannie handed her the plate. "Rough day?"

"It wasn't too bad."

"Miss Sadie says you did a right fine job of helping with Yellow Bird."

Ginger's eyebrows shot up. "She did?"

"Yep. She said not only did you help with the birth, but you stayed by Yellow Bird's side all day so that Miss Sadie could rest. She seemed awfully grateful."

Ginger accepted the praise but shook her head. "That

woman," she said. "She fussed at me every time I turned around."

Fannie laughed, returning to her work cleaning up around the campsite and washing dishes. "You know Miss Sadie isn't one to throw a compliment around. Especially not to the person she feels did a good job."

Ginger bit into her rabbit. She appreciated Fannie's friendship. Like Toni, the woman had welcomed her into the wagon train and accepted her without too much suspicion.

To be honest, she would like nothing more than to be able to confide in her about Web and the rest of the gang, but as the wagon master's wife, Fannie would be duty bound to let Blake know there were still outlaws in the area and that Ginger was raised by the ring leader. Even Toni would be forced to share her deception with Two Feathers. That's what people who were about to be married did—no secrets. So Ginger resigned herself to keeping her life before the wagon train, as well as her reunion with Web and his band of outlaws, firmly in her own memory. As much as she wanted to stay, she knew these people would never believe that she had nothing to do with the attack.

"I went by to see Yellow Bird earlier," Fannie said. "The baby is beautiful, isn't he?" Fannie's voice held a wistful tone that piqued Ginger's curiosity. Especially since, as far as she was concerned, the creature in Yellow Bird's arms was about the scrawniest mess of a human being she'd ever seen. "I guess so."

"You don't sound convinced," Fannie said, her lips curved into an amused smile.

Managing a shrug, Ginger swallowed down a bite of the wonderful meat. "Miss Sadie says all babies are odd looking when they first come. He'll get better, I guess."

Fannie chuckled. "Well anyway, I look forward to getting back on the trail tomorrow. Don't you? Just think—in a couple of months, we'll be in Oregon."

Ginger didn't really know how to respond. It was awfully hard to drum up any enthusiasm for Oregon when she most likely wouldn't be with the wagon train by the time they reached the so-called promised land.

"Okay, listen, Ginger." Fannie planted her hands on her hips and looked straight into Ginger's eyes. "I know you probably figure it's no use tryin' and that Blake is going to make you leave this time. And I'll be honest, he's mulling the idea around in that stubborn brain of his. But you still have a chance, if I know anything about what's in that man's head."

Swallowing, Ginger eyed the woman, almost afraid of the hope lifting her spirits. "You think I have a chance of staying?"

"I do. If you play your cards right. I don't mean to be vulgar, but neither of us was raised in a lady's parlor, were we? We understand the notion of playing the hand you're dealt but playing it smart."

Ginger might have laughed at the notion of being raised in a lady's parlor, if she weren't a bit offended. Not about the reference to gambling, of course—she'd won her fair share of money in one card game or another during her life. Lost her fair share too, truth be told. But why would Fannie assume she hadn't been raised by a lady? She'd never told one blessed person about her upbringing. Not even Toni and Fannie. "I guess I see your point."

"The key to managing Blake is to admit you're wrong and apologize before he starts yelling."

Ginger stiffened and jerked her chin. "What if I'm not wrong?"

"Depends on how important being right is to you."

It was just about everything to Ginger. "I'm not apologizing."

"Don't let your stubbornness get the better of you, Ginger. Blake's used to getting his way around this wagon train. And he's usually right." Fannie released a laugh that came straight from her belly. "Believe me, it took me a long time to admit it. I don't expect you to feel the same way about him, of course. As a matter of fact, you'd have a fight on your hands if I thought you'd taken a shine to my husband."

"Hey, now. I don't . . ."

"I was teasing about that, Ginger. I forgot how you take everything so literally."

Relief shoved her indignation back down.

Fannie obviously wasn't finished with her lecture. "The fact is, you might try to give in just a little in order to keep your place on the wagon train. I'd miss you something fierce if you had to go."

"You would?"

"Well, of course. And so would Toni and Miss Sadie." She sent her a conspiratorial grin. "And Grant Kelley."

Close to a growl, Ginger sent her a fierce scowl as she swallowed down the last of the rabbit meat from the bone. "Don't even mention his name to me."

"Why not? Surely you can't deny he's a right handsome man. Even a blind billy goat could see that."

"Can we please talk about something else?"

"Okay. Let's talk about how you're going to be so pleasant and apologetic that Blake feels downright hateful at the very thought of tossing you out on your behind. Oh, and you must promise never to disobey his orders again."

Ginger scowled. "Why can't they just leave me be to do what I want?"

All amusement fled Fannie's expression. "You already know the answer to that." She poured them each a cup of coffee from the tin pot on the fire grate. Walking back to Ginger, she handed her one of them and settled herself on the tongue of her wagon, facing Ginger. "The wagon train's success depends on everyone's cooperation. Surely you've seen that by now."

Ginger's face warmed under Fannie's scrutiny. She gathered her dignity and jerked her chin. "I do my part. Whatever chores I'm assigned. I just don't see why I can't ride off on my own if I want. Don't I always come back safe? And usually bagging meat enough for at least two or three families."

"That's very true. But you know as well as I do that a lone woman is a target for any number of threats. Animals, Indians. Or what about the attack this morning? Those men could still be in the area, just waiting to pick off the first fool who wanders away from the train."

Ginger had suddenly lost her appetite. Her defenses rose. "Only someone that can't take care of themselves is a fool."

Fannie shrugged, her eyes sparkling, obviously ready for

the conflict. "The Bible says someone who doesn't believe in God is a fool."

The words hit Ginger like a jolt. Now why would Fannie go and say a thing like that, right in the middle of a completely different conversation? "You saying I don't believe in God? Because I do. When Yellow Bird's babe wouldn't come out, we prayed and God answered."

"So you're saying if Yellow Bird and the baby had died, you would still believe there is a God?"

Well, when she put it that way it was hard to know how to answer. "I don't know. Maybe. But the fact is, He did like I asked."

Fannie gave her an indulgent smile and took the plate Ginger held out. "Glad to hear it. But you still shouldn't have ridden off alone. It's not about whether you can take care of yourself or not. Nor is it even about whether or not God will keep you safe. It's about the fact that Blake gave orders, and you disobeyed. It disrupted things around here. To tell you the truth, after the attack this morning and Yellow Bird's baby having trouble getting born, well . . . Blake didn't need one more thing to have to worry about."

Her somber words bit into Ginger, leaving her with remorse working its way from her stomach to her heart. "I guess when you put it that way . . ."

Fannie's lips curved into a smile. "Blake has told me more than once that you're a good tracker and have the potential to be one of the most valuable members of this entire train."

"Yeah?" Ginger's grin spread across her face in spite of herself.

Fannie leveled a frank gaze at her. "Yes, but he also says you're undisciplined and incapable of taking orders, and that's why he can't count on you. You're too unpredictable."

Ginger's smile faltered. "Oh." She stood. "I best go. Thank you for the supper. If Blake gets back, tell him I'm at my tent."

"All right. Try not to worry too much. You'll know Blake's decision soon enough."

Ginger tried to heed her friend's words, but it couldn't stop the tightening of her stomach. And she knew if she had to go, it was her own fault.

When they entered the supply tent, Blake nodded at Sam. "Good, you found Grant," Blake said, his tone grim.

Unease swept through Grant. "Something wrong, Blake?"

The wagon master motioned them to the back of the tent. They walked around crates and barrels. "Our scouts found this man, unconscious, in the woods."

A bedroll was stretched out against the back of the tent and on it laid a young man, probably no more than sixteen or seventeen years of age. His eyes were closed, and he shook with what Grant assumed was fever.

"Where was he found?"

Blake shook his head. "In the direction of the attack this morning. And it doesn't seem like he's been there all that long. His arm is broken. That's why we asked for you, Grant. Can you bandage him up? Looks like he fell off his horse and hit his head."

"I'll need some water and bandages for his head. And a couple of boards to make into a splint for his arm." He stopped and leveled a gaze at Blake. "He's also running a fever. We may be dealing with infection somewhere. I'll need to examine him thoroughly."

Blake nodded. "I'll ask Fannie to boil some water."

"I'll go," Sam spoke up.

Grant barely glanced his way. "Bring back a couple of boards so I can splint that arm, would you?"

Sam left to bring back the necessary items while Grant went to work.

After a brief examination, Grant was pretty sure Blake's suspicion was correct. The young man had fallen and hit his head. "Probably a rock," he said to Blake. "He's lucky he didn't knock his brains out. But the fever is what concerns me most. I don't find an infected wound. I can only assume he's ill."

A series of groans leaked from the unconscious stranger, as though he were trying to pull himself from the mire of his state and open his eyes.

Grant gripped his shoulder and held him steady on the pallet. "Take it easy. You're hurt."

Another groan and the man passed out again.

"He woke up once," Grant said. "Most likely he'll wake up again." At least he hoped so. Now that he was alone with the wagon master, his curiosity got the better of him. "I, uh, spoke with Ginger. She went looking for you."

"Stubborn female. I'll have a talk with her in the morning." He moved a horse blanket from a nearby crate and sat. Leaning forward, he rested his elbows on his thighs and heaved a sigh. "I just wish she hadn't forced this decision on me."

"You thinking of asking her to leave?"

"I'm not asking." The muscle in Blake's jaw twitched as he clenched his teeth.

Grant knew the girl deserved discipline, still, they could use every available gun. Besides, she had become a valuable part of the wagon train. Surely Blake could see that. Grant knew it wasn't his place to question the wagon master, but he couldn't seem to stuff the words back down his throat fast enough to keep them from flying out. "I guess you've thought it through?"

Blake straightened up and looked at Grant, eyes narrowed. "Is there some reason you think I shouldn't enforce our rules for this girl? She's been nothing but trouble, and you can't deny that. If I have my way, we'll drop her off at the first fort we come to. Of course, one more delay and we'll likely be forced to hole up at Fort Boise for the winter anyway."

Alert to the wagon master's concern, Grant shoved aside the thought of Ginger leaving the train and concentrated on the newly spoken situation. "The snows are already piling up in the mountains, aren't they?"

Blake scowled. "I don't know about snows piling up yet, but they most likely will be by the time we get there. We're more than a month behind. All the delays between women getting kidnapped, the twister, Indians, and now outlaws. This has been the worst trip west I've ever made. I'm glad it's my last."

"Is Fort Boise equipped to take on a wagon train the size of this one?"

"We'd have to build outside the fort and fortify the walls and roofs with wagon canvases."

"You mean build houses for folks?" Grant had trouble believing in the possibility.

Blake shook his head. "We'll have to build barracks, of sorts. Two for the women and girls, two for the men and boys."

"Splitting up families might not be good."

"We may not have a choice. Tepees would be more practical and would keep families together, but I know what kind of reaction I'd get if I suggested that sort of thing."

The man in the corner groaned, drawing their attention. Grant studied his young face.

"Can you hear me?" he asked.

The stranger moaned in reply but didn't open his eyes.

"Who are you?"

"Buddy . . ."

"What were you doing this close to the wagon train?"

"Gin-ger . . ." he whispered just before passing out once more.

"Confound it," Blake muttered. "I knew that girl was up to no good."

As much as Grant hated to admit it, there was no denying that Ginger was hiding something. "I guess we'd better send for her, huh?"

Sam entered the tent carrying two boards, water, and bandages.

Blake stood, raking his hand through his hair. "Set those down, Sam, and then will you go find Ginger Freeman? That fellow is asking for her."

A frown creased Sam's dark brow. "Asking for Ginger?"

As if on cue, the man stirred and moaned. "Ginger . . ."

"We're going to find her," Grant said. "But first I'm going to fix your broken arm and clean up the wound on your head. You're running a fever. Can you tell me if you've come into contact with influenza or any other infectious diseases lately?"

"Ch–cholera. In an Indian village south of here yesterday."

Grant turned and met Blake's gaze. The wagon master stared back gravely.

A wave of dread washed over Grant. Cholera had the capacity to wipe out the entire wagon train. He'd seen its devastating effects before. He looked down at the boy. First things first. He had to set the broken arm. Then he'd try to figure out how to keep the cholera from sweeping through camp.

Ginger's restlessness led her through camp after she left Fannie, and she found herself pausing outside of Miss Sadie's tent. "Hello!" she called.

"Come in, Ginger," Miss Sadie answered from inside.

Ginger rushed forward at the sight of Yellow Bird sitting up at the fire, nursing the baby. She coughed a little from the smoke. Even with a hole in the top of the tent where the stakes came together, almost as much smoke remained inside as escaped. But with the cold weather setting in, there was no choice but to build the fires or freeze. "Why are you up? You should be in bed." She turned her glare on Miss Sadie. "Aren't you supposed to be taking care of her? I knew I shouldn't have left Yellow Bird alone. I just knew it."

Outrage flashed in Miss Sadie's eyes. "Girl, I've been bringing babies and taking care of new mothers since before you were born. Do you think you know best?"

Warmth moved up Ginger's neck, but she refused to back down. Right was right. "I don't think she should be sitting up like that."

"The baby is finished now." A tired little smile tipped Yellow Bird's lips. She twisted her head and looked up. She patted the ground. "Come and tell me about your evening, Ginger. Where have you been? If you will hold him, I will lie down while you talk to me."

Well, she wasn't exactly experienced in baby holding, but she hadn't dropped him earlier, so she expected it wouldn't hurt anything to take on the little tyke so Yellow Bird would stretch out on her pallet. Expelling a breath, Ginger sank to the earthen floor across from Yellow Bird and held out her arms.

The first feel of the warm, swaddled babe in her arms touched a spot inside of Ginger, and she swallowed hard against a rush of emotion. His rosebud mouth scrunched up, and he let out a contented sigh as he stared up at her with black eyes. "Would you look at that?" Ginger said, barely able to gather enough breath to push the words from her throat.

"He knows you helped to bring him safely into the world," Yellow Bird said. Ginger couldn't summon the strength to look away from the wonder in her arms.

"You reckon?"

"I do. Babies are very wise."

Miss Sadie gave a snort. "You never answered Yellow

Bird's question. Where ya been? Grant's been pacing the length of the camp for hours. Making a nuisance of hisself."

"I went out riding. And Grant knew where I went. He tried to keep me from going."

Miss Sadie shook her head. "Riding? Didn't Blake say no one was to leave camp?"

"I didn't hear it."

"Well, even if you didn't. You know the routine by now. Only men are allowed away from camp during times like today. And even then, only in groups of two or more. Never a woman, and definitely never alone. And land sakes, not at night. What were you thinking?"

"I was thinking I had my reasons, and it was nobody's business what I do or don't do. And I hold to that belief." She glared at Miss Sadie. "You shouldn't talk that way in front of the baby, anyhow."

"Talk what way?"

"Land sakes," Ginger whispered so softly she practically just moved her lips.

"It is all right, Ginger," Yellow Bird said, "I do not think he understands words yet."

"Anyway, Fannie says Blake's just as likely to kick my be—" Glancing at the baby, she frowned. "Ask me to leave at Fort Boise as he is to let me stay."

Yellow Bird's eyes shone with sympathy. "You are like water just before it slips over the fall."

That Yellow Bird was a curiosity. Sometimes she might as well be speaking Sioux, for all the sense she made. "What are you talking about, Yellow Bird?"

The Indian woman cast her an indulgent smile. "Neither can be contained." Her gaze shifted to the now-sleeping baby. "I will take him now."

Reluctantly, Ginger settled the baby into his mother's arms.

"Neither can be contained," Miss Sadie mimicked Yellow Bird's words. "That's what a dam is for." She handed Ginger a cup of coffee she hadn't even asked for. Ginger took it gratefully, anticipating the warmth. "Thanks. It's getting downright cold."

The widow's face softened. "Heaven help the person who tries to dam up your energy, my girl."

Ginger sipped the hot liquid, then swallowed. "Think Blake's gonna kick me out?"

Miss Sadie's shoulders lifted in a shrug. "He might. You seem to have a knack for getting into trouble."

Ginger opened her mouth to protest, but Miss Sadie silenced her with an upraised hand. She placed the pot back on the fire. "Hold on. I'm not done. What I was going to say, is that you also have a knack for helping folks around here. More often than not, your hunting and fishing skills keep meat on several fires around camp. I'm sure Blake will take that into consideration before making a decision."

"I hope so, Miss Sadie." Ginger shoved the cup back in to the older woman's hand and headed toward the tent flap. "I'll stop by in the morning to help get Yellow Bird settled in the back of your wagon. Get some sleep, Yellow Bird. The trail gets rougher tomorrow. You won't rest in the wagon."

"Thank you, Ginger I will sleep soon."

"All right, then." She gave a nod that included both women. "I'll say goodnight."

Ginger walked outside into the chilly air, grateful to be out of the smoky tent. She turned her gaze toward the west. It was almost November. The wagon train should have been in Oregon Territory by now, but one delay after another had slowed their progress. It would be a miracle if they made it through the mountains ahead before the winter set in. Otherwise, she didn't know if she could hold Web off that long. He was mighty determined she should hurry and get back to him and the rest of the gang. What could he've meant about needing a woman for their next scheme? Well, whatever it was, he could forget it. She hadn't been part of Web's thieving and such for seven years, and she wasn't going to go back to it now. Even if it meant that she left her pa forever. Then again, Web had seemed anxious. What if he left her no choice?

When she returned to her campfire, she found Sam waiting. His lips were set in a grim line, his eyes void of humor.

"Hi Sam, what are you doing?"

He nodded. "I was sent to bring you to the supply tent. A young man has been brought in wounded. He called your name."

Four

Ginger's legs shook as she walked with Sam toward the supply tent. By the description Sam had given of the young man, it could only be Buddy. Frustration bit at her. How could her brother be so foolish? If what Two Feathers said was true, he had given her away.

Just how much Buddy had told, she couldn't be sure so she didn't allow herself to speak. But if he'd so much as hinted that he had been involved in the attack this morning, Web was as good as found. With Sam's and Grant's abilities as trackers, it wouldn't be long before they rounded up the rest of Web's gang, and the whole lot of them—including Ginger—would be in a mess of trouble.

Her stomach quivered as she slipped through the tent flap.

Standing quickly from Buddy's bedside, Grant held up his arms. "Get her out of here. This man has cholera."

A gasp shuddered through Ginger. She pushed past him. "You're not keeping me from my brother. Especially if he's sick."

"Your brother?" Blake asked, suspicion edging his voice.

Ginger nodded. "Yes. His name is Buddy. He . . . he must have followed me west." She reached forward and brushed a lock of Buddy's brown hair from his forehead.

Grant placed a hand on her shoulder. "Ginger, if this is cholera, you've just exposed yourself to the disease by touching him. You're risking your life and the lives of others by that stunt you just pulled."

Ginger examined her younger brother's sweet boyish face. He shivered under the thin blanket covering him and his brow was damp with sweat. Just like Web's had been earlier.

Blake nodded to Grant. "She's already exposed herself now. We might as well get some answers. Wake him up."

Grant waved smelling salts under Buddy's nose. The young man sniffed, jerked, and came awake with a start.

Without so much as a nod at Ginger, Blake looked at Buddy. "Ginger's here, just like we promised. Ginger, look at me."

She turned to face the wagon master. Blake's eyes demanded answers. "Whether he's sick or not, I have to know if he has anything to do with that band of outlaws that attacked our train."

Buddy's eyes grew wide as he looked to Ginger to see how much she would admit to. Ginger hated to lie, but she couldn't betray her brother. He was barely fifteen years old. How could she hand him over to Blake to be hanged? On the trail, justice was swift and administered by the hands of those in charge. This far from a town with a sheriff, there was no other choice. Just as she had no choice now but to protect her brother.

"Outlaw?" She forced a laugh. "My Buddy? Does he look like an outlaw?"

Grant narrowed his gaze. Ginger swallowed hard but raised her chin against his disbelief. "Buddy always said if I ran off, he'd follow me." That much was true. "Didn't you?"

"Yeah," he muttered, closing his eyes.

"Is that the truth, son?" Grant asked.

"You calling my brother a liar?"

"No."

Grant's curt reply and knowing gaze silenced Ginger. She swallowed hard. How was she ever going to get out of this mess without Buddy and possibly herself swinging from the end of a rope?

The scowl on Grant's face made it clear he wasn't going to budge, no matter what she said. "Look, Blake," she said, appealing to the wagon master. "My brother is sick and obviously alone. He came looking for me, that's all. I'm the only family he's got since our ma abandoned us."

"What about your pa?"

Ginger gave a snort. "Pa? Web's about the sorriest excuse for a pa you ever could see. We're better off without him."

"She's telling the truth about that," Buddy said in a meek voice that concerned Ginger. How sick was he? Her knees went soft at the thought of Buddy dying a horrible death of cholera.

"Buddy, lay still and let me take care of this, will you?" She studied his pale face with a frown. "You feeling okay?"

"I feel awful sick, Ginger."

Grant stepped forward. "All right. Enough of this for

now. Whatever the reason for this young man's appearance, the fact is he's ill. I need someone to bring me a bucket, and I'll need all the quinine I can get my hands on just in case this thing spreads."

Blake looked from Ginger to Buddy and back to Grant. "I guess I don't really have much of a choice."

Blake took her arm. "Come with me."

Grant stepped forward. "Wait, Blake. We need to inform the people that cholera is among us. Sam and you have already been in the tent and back out, so there's no containing it now. Whoever you came in contact with has also been exposed and has in turn exposed anyone else they've been close to. Tell them to watch for fever, vomiting, diarrhea."

Blake nodded. "We'll get the word out." He turned to Sam. "Take the west side of camp. I'll take the east. We'll spread the word among the captains, and they can tell their people."

He turned back to Ginger. "I need to have a word with you."

Ginger knew better than to try to pull away. She nodded. "I'll be back, Buddy," she called over her shoulder, although he appeared to have passed out. Once they ducked through the tent flap and stood outside, Blake turned her loose. They faced each other, Blake's square-shouldered stance firm and allowing for no backtalk.

"Now, what do you have to say for yourself?"

Ginger fought a rising panic. She didn't know what she was supposed to explain, exactly—Buddy's presence, or her riding out without permission?

Besides, his high-and-mighty tone irked her. She matched him look for look. "About what?"

"You know what I'm talking about," he growled. "Why did you ride off after I ordered that no one was to leave camp?"

Ginger watched the puff of air accompanying his words, as she sought to lasso a believable thought. Still, the familiar excuse flew out of her mouth, as though she hadn't thought about it at all. "I just needed to ride."

Between his eyes, two lines formed a deep frown. "What do you mean, you just needed to ride?"

A shrug lifted her shoulders. She wanted to tell him to mind his own business—that if she wanted to ride and try to ease the knot in her stomach, she should be allowed to do so. But with Buddy ill, hurt, and possibly dying, she especially couldn't take any chances that Blake would toss her out of the train. "I just needed to be alone."

He narrowed his eyes and peered closer. "Where did you go?"

Ginger jerked her thumb toward the west. "That way."

"Did you meet anyone or see signs of the attackers?"

For once, Ginger hesitated and weighed her words carefully. Buddy's presence proved that she had people in the vicinity. Still, she couldn't very well admit her connection to the attackers. So, she did the next best thing.

"I saw my pa."

"What do you mean? I thought you said you and Buddy were alone in the world."

"We said we have a pa. Just not a very good one."

Blake nodded as his eyes registered the memory. "And

your pa and Buddy showing up the same day a band of out-laws attacks the wagon train is nothing but a coincidence?"

Now that he put it that way, Ginger realized the only way to get out of this mess was to pretend innocence. "That's right. Just an odd coincidence." Ginger's lips turned up in what she hoped was a convincing smile.

"If you don't care much for your pa, what's he doing in these parts?"

"He was looking for Buddy." Now that wasn't exactly a lie. After all, Web did mention that her brother was missing. "Asked me if I'd seen him, but I didn't know Buddy was looking for me at the time, so I had to tell him no."

"And there was no one else with your pa?"

In a moment that could only be attributed to providence, Grant ducked through the tent flap at the very second Ginger would have either had to admit what she was or tell another lie; neither option appealed to her.

"How's Buddy?" she asked, aware that her voice was a little breathless—a telltale sign that she was relieved and evading Blake's question.

His lips held in a grim line, and he shook his head.

Fear gripped Ginger. "Grant?"

"You should probably prepare for the worst. He's very ill, and cholera is a fast killer."

Ginger tried to wrap her mind around his words, but her heart rejected the very thought that she could possibly lose another brother. "But Miss Sadie had it," Ginger said. "She didn't die."

Grant peered closer. "Are you sure about that?"

"Yes. Her sons and husband died of it. That's why she came west."

"Then she might be able to help if this thing sweeps through the wagon train. In the meantime, I've given him something to help with the pain," Grant told her.

"Can I see him again before I turn in?"

Grant shook his head. "Let him rest, Ginger. The boy is very ill."

"But why can't I stay with him? You said yourself that I'm already exposed."

"You need to get your rest. Stay strong, just in case you do get sick."

Resigned, Ginger nodded. "All right. But I'm coming back in the morning." She turned to Blake. "Are you finished with me for tonight?"

So far, he hadn't mentioned a punishment of leaving camp, but she was sure he was building up to it. "We're finished for tonight," Blake said. "But I expect you to follow orders from now on, and as punishment, you are off the scouting detail until further notice. That means no tracking, no hunting. And most of all, no leaving the wagon train for any reason."

Ginger opened her mouth to protest, but Grant placed a gentle, silencing hand on her arm. She nodded. "All right." After all, she had more important things to think about.

Blake shoved a finger toward her. "Until further notice, you're on water detail."

Indignation filled her chest. "Water detail!" Punishment was one thing, but he didn't have to insult her!

"Would you prefer to gather buffalo chips for the fire?"

Ginger stepped back quickly. "I'll fetch water."

"Good." Blake gave a nod. "Report to Miss Sadie at daybreak."

Miss Sadie was in charge of several chores—collecting chips, water, and anytime there was a camp-wide hunting expedition, she divvied up the meat.

Ginger said goodnight and headed back to the tent she shared with Toni. Her friend offered her a cup of coffee when she arrived. Ginger nodded gratefully. "Thanks."

"So what was Blake's punishment?"

"Water detail," she said glumly.

Toni gave a short laugh. "That's my every day chore. But I can see why you'd consider it a punishment." She handed Ginger the tin cup. "Sam stopped by. He said you have a visitor in camp."

"Not exactly a visitor. He's my brother, and he's apparently got cholera."

"Sam told me. I'm so sorry."

"Grant wouldn't let me stay with him." She took a sip of her coffee, then bended forward to rest her forearms on her knees. She studied the cup she cradled between her hands. "He told me to rest. How does he expect me to do that when my baby brother is in the supply tent all alone?"

"He's just looking out for you, Ginger," Toni soothed. "It's what he does."

"I don't need him looking out for me. I need him to let me look out for Buddy."

"Well, I think we'd all better get ready. Cholera isn't going to go away quietly. The next couple of weeks are going to be more than hard for everyone."

For the first time, Ginger considered the implications of this disease beyond her brother. "You think a lot of people are going to die?"

"Sam seemed concerned. And I've seen this disease before. It isn't going to be pretty."

"Blake and Sam are out warning folks now."

"I hope it doesn't cause a panic."

Ginger gave a shrug. "I reckon Blake knows what he's doing."

Toni rinsed out the coffeepot. A yawn stretched her mouth. "Are you ready to turn in?"

"I'll just dump out the wash water and take care of the fire, then I'll be in."

Nodding, Toni said goodnight and ducked into the tent.

Alone, Ginger extinguished the campfire, feeling the darkness swirling around her.

A shudder ran down her spine. Maybe it was her imagination, but she could feel eyes on her, watching. She stopped and turned quickly. "Web?" she whispered. Maybe he was checking on Buddy after all.

But silence answered. Her heart beat faster and she resumed her walk, quickening her steps, anxious to reach her tent and escape the feeling of those prying eyes.

Grant thought about Ginger as he administered quinine to the boy lying on the pallet in the supply tent. He'd watched her walk away, her body held with much less confidence than he was accustomed to seeing from her. Her head drooped just a little, and her gait seemed a bit slower, less cocky. Her brother's appearance and illness had most assuredly upset her. He didn't blame her. He himself was terrified, if he had to be honest about it. When Blake returned later with some supplies, Grant finally gave in to his curiosity. "What did she have to say for herself?"

"About riding off alone?" Blake shrugged. "The usual. Just needed to get alone. I understand how she feels. There are times when I'd like to ride off on Dusty and not come back until we're both sweating buckets and I feel my head clear. But I can't allow that sort of thing. If everyone ran off whenever they took a notion to, we'd have no discipline around here."

Grant nodded. "I agree. Did Ginger have an explanation for her brother showing up out of nowhere?"

"Nothing more than what she already said. She did say that she ran into her pa while she was out there today."

"Her pa?" Somehow, Grant didn't find this news too shocking. Not after her brother had appeared out of nowhere. Even a man of faith would have trouble believing such a thing were mere coincidence or simply an ambitious fifteen-year-old brother traveling alone, all the way from Missouri just to find her. "Do you think there's a connection between this morning's attack and Ginger's reunion with her pa and brother?"

"Only a fool would think otherwise."

Grant nodded in agreement. Blake was no fool. Grant walked next to him as they made their way through camp. "I figure she's seen more than just her pa and her brother."

"I'd put money on it." Blake dropped his tone. "As a matter of fact, I'm banking on Ginger's presence in the wagon train to draw them out." His gaze swept the camp. "I told the captains of each section to double the guards for each section of the train."

Grant nodded. "What about the scouts? Should we double them, too?"

"Makes sense. Numbers might discourage an attack. Let them go in groups of three, at daybreak. If there are any tracks ahead, I want them found before the wagons rolls over them." He gathered a deep breath. "I don't want any more surprise attacks."

"Something else to consider," Grant said. "It's possible more than just Ginger's brother has come down with cholera."

Blake scowled and nodded. "The thought has crossed my mind, as well. Unless we can get her to admit to being part of that outfit, how do we flush them out before they spread it to anyone else?"

"She may need to be confronted."

All in all, Grant knew that Ginger had a good heart. She might not turn in her pa if it meant him going to jail or getting hanged, but he couldn't believe she'd want to be responsible for unnecessary deaths.

At least not if she was the kind of young woman he believed her to be. He just hoped he wasn't wrong about her.

Web eyed his opponent, sizing him up like he would anyone who dared question his authority. "Like I said, we're waitin' this thing out."

Lane shook his head, refusing to back down. "We've got to leave these parts or we're gonna get ourselves caught." His words carried across camp. Web sensed the tension in his men. They weren't used to outbursts such as this one. Web's word was law, and that was that. Even those who disagreed rarely said so. And if they did, they sure didn't say it twice. So why, all of a sudden was the one man he thought he could count on betraying him?

Throughout his years as leader of this band of outcasts and outlaws, Web had been challenged before and had always dealt with the upstart in his own way. This time was different. Lane's silver-talking tongue had earned him sway with some of the men. But as far as Web knew, they were still loyal to him. For now, anyway. He needed to appeal to their sense of loyalty. And he needed to do it fast. If this stomach ailment was what he suspected, he and two other men in camp had contracted cholera from them Indians.

"Listen, men." Web held up his hand and moved in next to Lane. "A half-day's ride away is plenty far away from the wagon train. Even the trackers won't ride too far from the rest of the group. They're more concerned with immediate danger. As long as we keep our distance, we need to stick with the plan."

Lane shook his head and raised his voice. "Don't be fooled by Web! He's only saying that because he has Buddy and Ginger both in that camp. You know they're spying for him right now."

"What?" Web shouted, his head swimming with dizziness. The fact was, he wished he'd thought of planting a spy.

He could shoot himself for not, as a matter of fact. He didn't know where Buddy was, and he wasn't sure whether Ginger was still loyal to him or not.

"Lane, you know as well as I do that Buddy ain't nowhere near that wagon train."

"Really? Then where is he, Web?" Lane's brow rose in challenge.

"Well, I don't rightly know that. He went looking for his sister—that's true—but he ain't daft enough to walk into camp and start callin' her name."

"Well, I happen to know he is in their camp."

Web narrowed his gaze at the man. In the back of his mind, he thought about Lane riding into camp late with a few rabbits slung across his saddle.

Lane's horse had been ridden harder than he let on. And harder than anyone would ride on a hunt.

Web leveled his gaze at Lane. "You been spying on the wagon train without letting me know about it?"

Lane nodded. "I saw him. He must have hurt himself, because they carried him into camp. It looked like he was unconscious. Seems like they must have found out he's connected to Ginger, because they took her to the tent where they're holding him."

The news slammed into Web's gut, and he fought to keep from retching. He swallowed hard and gathered his composure. "Who told you to hang back and spy on my girl? You plannin' on doublecrossin' me?"

Lane's desire for Ginger had been common knowledge since she was fourteen years old and began displaying wom-

anly qualities. Common knowledge, that was, except to
Ginger. She was oblivious to anything romantic. Just as well.
Without a mother, she'd been raised in a man's world. To
her credit, she didn't have any evil feminine wiles, but also
no feminine instincts that he'd ever observed. Her worthless mother had seen to that. The woman never was much
of a mother—or a wife, for that matter. But whether Ginger
knew Lane was sweet on her or not, he still didn't have any
call to sneak around and gawk at her without her knowing.
It just wasn't right.

"Did you hear me, boy?" he said. "What was you doin',
staying back when the rest of us moved on?"

A lazy smile collected at the corner of Lane's mouth.
"That's my business, I reckon."

In a flash, Web snatched the front of Lane's shirt and
yanked him forward. Fear replaced insolence, and the
younger man's eyes widened.

"I'm makin' it my business, you two-bit idiot." A wave of
nausea swarmed his gut, but he fought it back.

Elijah stepped forward and spread his hands. "Let's not fight
amongst ourselves. I'm sure it hasn't escaped anyone's notice
that James and Murray are ailing. I'm guessing cholera. Do you
think we ought to be concentrating on not spreading it?"

Web turned Lane loose with a jolt. "Elijah's got a point.
Now, I don't want to hear any more. A half-day's ride is
plenty far away. Anyone else what to challenge me?"

Web knew he was on dangerous ground when someone
like Lane, who had ridden with him since he was just a boy,

could go against him for no good reason. The other men would lose confidence if he didn't do something quick.

He turned to the rest of the men, who stood in silence, waiting, watching to see what he would do. "Now, you men know me. Have I ever led you into anything that wasn't for the good of the entire gang?"

Murmurs of assent buzzed around the group. Confidence surged through Web. "All right then. I have my reasons for not riding away just yet."

Lane seemed unable to let well enough alone. "Seems to me, if we're going to risk our necks for your so-called reasons, you ought to come clean to the rest of us."

Web knew if he gave in to Lane's demands he would be in danger of losing his command of this ragtag bunch of misfits that he had pulled together and made into a family. And he couldn't let that happen. His biggest regret at the moment was ever treating Lane like a son. Still, he figured he'd best remind the men just why they'd left Missouri and followed the wagon train. It was his only defense against Lane's poison.

"Remember why we hit the wagon train in the first place?" He leveled his gaze and scrutinized the whole lot of ungrateful idiots. "Who joined the wagon train the same time as Grant Kelley?" He hesitated a moment for effect. "Harrison. Charles Harrison. Richest fella in Kansas. And ain't we lucky that he packed up, lock, stock, and barrel, and decided to head west with that idiot son of his, a pretty wife, and young daughter? How many of you got enough brains to figure out what he probably didn't leave behind?"

"His money?"

Poor Yuley. He was as slow as Harrison's son. His big grin flashed proudly.

Web clapped the simpleton on the shoulder with parental approval. "That's right, Yuley. His money. Now, how many of you want to ride off and leave all those thousands of dollars that I just bet are under a false bottom or in their supply wagon, locked away in a box?"

No one raised a hand. He turned in triumph to Lane. "I guess you got your answer. If you ever go against my word again, I'll put a bullet in you."

Lane's eyes darkened further. "I don't like threats."

"And I don't like my leadership questioned. Now, this was my outfit from the start, and I don't mean to hand it over to the likes of you before I'm good and ready." He paused for a breath. "Unless I change my mind and hand it over to someone else."

"All right. Your point is taken. But tell me, how do you plan to get us close enough to find the box and then steal it?"

"I'll let you know tomorrow."

Because the fact of the matter was that Web had no idea how he was going to manage to grab the money and make sure his young'uns were safe. The best he could do right now was get away by himself somewhere and think on it a bit. He walked away from camp. But not so far that he couldn't keep the campfire in sight. Lane would like nothing better than to catch him out alone and do him in. The longer he walked the more he thought about Lane until he came to a sober conclusion. With the traitor's poison spreading through the group,

Web had no choice but to find out once and for all where Ginger's loyalties lay. He couldn't care less about whether or not she ever put a bullet in that doctor. In a raid, men on either side would be killed, and no one was to blame. War was war. And he didn't believe in revenge. It was a waste of time. Only once had he given in to bloodlust. That was his secret, and he'd never do it again.

He would enter the camp and introduce himself as Ginger's Pa that had been looking for his girl. She had friends there. If they trusted her, they'd surely trust her pa. It wouldn't take long to make friends with Harrison and find out about the money. Then Ginger could do what she needed to do, and they could grab the money and be on their way before anyone was the wiser. It was time to get on with the new plan. Ginger wouldn't be happy with her role, but she had no choice.

A grim smile slowly stretched his mouth as he imagined the entire plan in his mind.

Tonight, he would sleep like a baby. And in the morning, he'd join the wagon train and reunite with his two children. Hopefully, his stomach would settle down by then.

Five

Ginger made her way through camp toward the supply tent where Buddy was kept, hoping she wouldn't be noticed in the bustle of nighttime activities. She'd hated to lie to Toni, but the only way to get out of the tent was to pretend she needed to go and do her business. The kind of business a person had to do alone.

Earlier, she'd heard Blake instruct Two Feathers to post one guard at the entrance to the supply tent. That was a mercy. Getting past one guard wouldn't be much of a challenge. Especially when that guard was Nate Lyons—not the smartest man Sam could have chosen to keep watch.

She figured Grant would have gone back to his own tent by now. And she was determined that her brother wasn't going to die while she slept in her warm tent. As she approached, she changed her course, snatching up a stone as she tiptoed around to the back of the tent. Aiming carefully away from the tent, she tossed the rock a few feet from Nate. He turned his head sharply—just as she'd intended. Predictably, when the sound didn't immediately repeat, he retook his position and looked straight ahead. Ginger tossed another stone and another one. Nate took the bait. "Who's there?"

Cautiously, he walked toward the sound and away from his post, which would most likely get him a firm tongue lashing from Sam or Blake. A fact that made Ginger feel a little guilty, but not enough to stop her from her mission to get inside that tent where her brother was being kept. She stealthily moved along the cloth wall, making her way around the front. She ducked inside without being spotted.

She should thank her lucky stars that Nate was missing a few brains. Anyone smarter wouldn't have been fooled. As a matter of fact, she'd been meaning to speak to Blake about Nate's incompetence. Now she was glad it had slipped her mind.

"Buddy," she whispered. "You awake?"

"Yeah," came the returning whisper. "Boy, am I ever glad to see you. They tied me up. It hurts somethin' fierce. Can you cut me loose?"

Indignation flashed through her as she observed his precarious position. Poor Buddy's uninjured arm was stretched across his body where both arms could meet at the wrists. "Barbarians," she said, blinking back tears of pity at what she knew had to be excruciating pain. "Hang on, Buddy, I'll have you out of that knot in a hurry" She knelt beside his pallet and yanked her hunting knife from her belt.

Buddy gazed up at her, his blue eyes filled with worry. "It won't get you into any trouble will it?" His voice sounded so weak, Ginger fought the urge to tear up. How could anyone tie up a boy that was not only hurt but also so sick? Just wait until she got her hands on that idiot Grant. He would have been the last person to see Buddy. It had to have been him.

"Let it. I'm going to cut you loose. My brother isn't going to be tied up like an animal." She gave a bitter laugh. "Worse than an animal. The horses and oxen roam free. How are you feeling?"

"Awful, Ginger," he said, moaning. "I think I'm gonna die."

"Don't you dare say that, you hear?" The blade made short work of Buddy's bindings. He sighed and rubbed his shoulder where it had been stretched.

"Thanks," he mumbled as though speaking was too much effort.

Brushing aside his thanks, Ginger adjusted her position so that she sat cross-legged on the ground next to his pallet. "What were you doing out there, Buddy? Why did you stay behind after Web and the rest of the gang rode off?"

His eyes remained closed. "I told you . . ." he said weakly.

Memory washed over her, taking her back four months to late spring. Buddy had held Tulip's halter and stared up at her as he said, "If you don't get home before harvest, I'm coming after you."

Funny how they measured time the same way the farmers in Missouri did. How often had Ginger gone to bed in some rowdy, bawdy house or shivering in the cold of a winter camp, wished for a home with parents who tilled the ground, planted, and brought in the harvest? Honest pay for an honest day's work. She and Buddy used to lay close and dream aloud about the sort of man their dream pa might be. Their dream ma. All they'd had was each other. And Clem.

Someone had brought in a washbasin of water and strips of cloth. She dipped the cloth and squeezed. "How'd you know I was with the wagon train?"

"Web." He closed his eyes, and his face took on peace as Ginger pressed the cool cloth against his feverish forehead.

Ginger shook her head at a stinging realization. Even though Web had assumed she was with the wagon train, he hadn't thought twice about raiding them? He either hadn't thought about the possibility of someone's bullet connecting with her skull, or it was a risk he'd been willing to take. Probably the latter.

More troublesome, though, was the fact that Buddy was in the middle of the whole thing. "You were part of the raid?" Buddy had never done anything illegal. If he had ridden with Web's people and drawn a gun, he was guilty, too.

He shook his head once. "Snuck off to find you." He moaned, the sound tugging on Ginger's heart.

"Don't try to talk anymore, Buddy. You need to save your strength."

"One more thing . . . The doctor . . . he's a good man."

Ginger released a deep sigh. "He is. I know he is." It was the first time Ginger had admitted such a thing—even to herself. But hearing the words from her brother's lips, she knew he was speaking the truth. And he'd only known the man a few hours.

The more Ginger saw things with this new perspective, she realized that no matter what had happened that day so long ago, she wasn't unreasonable enough not to realize the man was mourning his own wife. No one but an out-and-out saint would have dragged himself away from his wife to help one of the men responsible for her death. She knew that now. Still, there was a lot at stake. She dipped the cloth in the cool water and swiped it across Buddy's forehead. "Grant is a good man, Buddy. I've known him long enough to understand that. He would never willingly let a man die. But you have to remember not to let on where we come from. If he knew who we are, he wouldn't be lifting a hand to help. Remember—his wife died in that raid."

"Ginger, I need . . ." Buddy's eyes shot to the bucket. She grabbed it just in time and held it until he was finished.

"Lay still. I'll tend you."

She rubbed the wet towel across his forehead. His face was devoid of color and his skin clammy. His eyes closed, and she knew he'd fallen asleep. Ginger set the towel back in the basin of water and stretched out on the hard ground a few inches away from her brother's pallet. She rested her head on her bent elbow.

"God," she whispered. "Please don't let Buddy die. He's all I have left."

She watched the steady rise and fall of Buddy's chest as he slept. How many times had they fallen asleep this way over the last fifteen years? Too many to count, she figured. Before her older brother, Clem, died, he would lay down with her much the same way she did Buddy. Keeping her safe, making sure no harm came to her. And none ever had. Clem had taught her to ride, to shoot, to trap and fish. He might as well have been her pa. Without question, he was more of a pa than Web ever was.

If only Clem were still alive. He had promised her. One

last robbery—the stagecoach bound for St. Louis. And he would take his cut and the three of them would go to Texas, start a new life, maybe on a ranch of their own. Clem had fed into her big dreams of someday being a respectable citizen. Only instead of all of her dreams coming true that day, her worst nightmare had occurred. Clem had been shot by the driver of the stagecoach. But he might have made it if the doctor on board the stagecoach had helped him.

Pain squeezed her heart at the memory. Clem's death was as much her fault as the doctor who had let him bleed to death on the Missouri prairie. She had played the decoy, had stood in the road and waited for the stage to come. She waved them down and of course they'd stop for her just like all the others.

This particular ploy had worked too many times for Web to consider the possibility that the time might come when their tactics would fail. As she thought back on it, she supposed it was like Sam Two Feathers said during his last Sunday sermon around Toni's campfire when he described the giant crashing to the earth, defeated by a small shepherd boy with a sling and a stone. "Pride goeth before a fall."

Web's pride in the way they'd profited that summer led him to be careless. When the stage driver pulled in the reins and everyone inside was distracted by Ginger's sudden appearance, Web and his gang rode hard from the woods, shooting into the air to create chaos and confusion. It had worked a hundred times, but this time the robbery went bad.

How could they have known there was a US Marshal on the stage? The fighting was hot, but when the smoke cleared,

Web and the boys took off, leaving Ginger behind and Clem bleeding on the ground from a gut shot.

"Sarah!" The scream coming from within the stage, mirrored the horror Ginger felt as she threw herself to the ground and lay across Clem's heaving chest. The stage door flew open and a man jumped out, pulling a woman with him. "Bring my bag!" he yelled to no one in particular as he gently lowered her to the ground. "My bag!"

"Don't bother." Another man appeared, this one wearing a badge. "She was dead the second that bullet hit her."

"I'm a doctor. I can save her. I have to save my wife!"

Ginger's heart had lifted with hope that only a child can muster in situations like that one. "Hang on, Clem. Please, hang on. There's a doctor."

"Don't." He'd barely gotten the strength to speak. "He won't help. I don't blame him. I'm good as dead, Ginger. I'm sorry about the ranch. Take care of Buddy."

"Hang on, Clem," she'd sobbed. "I'll be back."

"No. Don't. Get out of here fast."

But Ginger hadn't listened. She'd never leave him. Soaked in her brother's blood, she ran toward the doctor. "Help me, please."

The man's brown eyes had lifted silently to hers. Dazed. "What?"

Fear had hit her squarely the second she saw the pain and anger in his face. "My—my brother. We got caught in that fight. The dirty outlaws shot my brother!"

"I don't think so, girlie," the Marshal had said with a sneer. "He's one of 'em. And looks like you are, too."

Her brother groaned. Ginger clenched her fist as the panic turned to desperation. She grabbed the doctor's shoulders and shook. "That woman's dead, but my brother isn't. I need help!"

Agony clouded his eyes. "That woman is my wife," he'd murmured.

But Ginger hadn't cared who she was. The only thing that mattered was Clem. He had to make it. "Hurry!" she called to Grant. "He's dying! Don't let my brother die!" But it was no use.

And now Buddy lay sick. Another brother at Grant's mercy. She knew Grant was doing everything in his power, but the situation itself brought the memories and the pain as though it were yesterday. When she looked down at Buddy, with his dark brown hair than fell over his ears in unruly waves, it was as though she were looking at Clem himself. Even the scraggly whiskers along his jaw mirrored Clem's. Would he get the chance to become a man? Her sweet Buddy. He couldn't die. He just couldn't. In the darkness of the tent, Ginger prayed harder than she'd ever prayed before.

Grant woke with a start to the sound of footsteps creeping close. His hand went instinctively to the revolver at his side.

"Grant?" a woman's voice whispered into the night. "Are you in there? It's Toni."

Anticipating possible trouble from the outlaws, Grant was fully dressed, including his boots. He was on his feet before he answered, "I'm awake."

As he stepped outside, he was greeted by Toni's worried face. "Ginger's missing."

"What do you mean missing?" he asked, his stomach dropping. "As in someone took her, or as in she wandered off alone again?"

"I honestly don't know. But it's very late, and she's not back yet."

"Do you know when she left?"

"Over two hours ago. She said she had to . . . well, you know . . ." Toni ducked her head as he drew the obvious conclusion.

"You waited two hours to come tell me? Didn't you realize she wasn't coming back?"

"I'm sorry, Grant." Her voice trembled with agony and self-condemnation. "I guess I fell asleep, because when I woke up the fire had gone completely out, and it was cold inside our tent."

Grant slapped his hat on his head. He'd love to shake Ginger. He shot a glance at Toni. "You've done all you can. Go back to your tent. I'll look for her."

Relief crossed her features. "Thank you. I probably should have gone to Sam or Blake, but either of them would have been too hard on her."

"What makes you think I won't be?"

A soft smile tilted her lips. "Because you care for her."

Grant frowned at her words. "I do care for her—like I do all of the members of the wagon train. If she's run off, I'll have to report back to Blake. She's walking a fine line as it is. I can't keep this from him."

"I understand." She placed a hand on his arm. "Don't be too hard on her, Grant. I have a feeling Ginger hides a lot of pain. Sometimes, I think she has to be alone because it's the only time she feels free."

He drew a sharp breath at the thought of what might have caused Ginger the kind of deep down pain that would jeopardize her position on the wagon train over and over.

"Goodnight, Miss Toni. I'll keep an eye on you until you get back."

After she'd made it safely back to the tent she shared with Ginger, he headed toward the makeshift corral to saddle up his horse. When he got there, he realized Ginger couldn't have ridden off because Tulip was still penned up with the rest of the livestock. He frowned. Where was that girl?

Then it hit him. He felt stupid for not anticipating her move. His feet made quick steps toward the supply tent, half-expecting to see the guard knocked out on the ground. When he arrived, however, he stopped short at the sight of Nate standing dutifully, rifle over shoulder, guarding the tent.

"Doc." Nate inclined his head. "Come to see your patient?"

Grant nodded. He pushed his hat higher on his head with two fingers. "Has anyone else tried to see him tonight?"

"Nope. Not since you patched him up and left yourself earlier. Why?"

"No reason. And yeah, I've come to check on him."

"You go right on ahead." He moved toward the flap to open it for Grant, then he looked up. "You don't got to worry about him going for you. I tied his hands and feet together so he couldn't attack anyone."

Grant's eyes narrowed as he digested the words. "You did what?"

"Tied up the prisoner."

Grant fought hard not to punch that pleased look off Nate's face. Instead, he peered closer, leaving no question in his stern expression and firm tone that he was less than satisfied with the news.

"By whose authority did you tie up a prisoner you were instructed only to guard? You weren't supposed to enter the tent, let alone initiate contact."

Nate's grin faded. "I—I thought . . . that is, I thought I'd be able to guard him better if he couldn't jump me the second my back was turned."

"The man has a broken arm, and judging from the size of the knot he received falling off his horse, I'd say he's got a concussion. Sleep is going to be on his agenda tonight. Trust me, he's in no shape to get the jump on anyone."

"Well, I'm truly sorry, Doc. I didn't know. But I was careful of that arm and tried not to hurt him. He stretched the other one over so I could tie them together."

"That's very decent of you," Grant muttered, sarcasm dripping off the words. "I'll be going inside now. Do not tie up my patient again."

"Yes sir."

Grant hated to cause a panic, but Nate would have to be isolated now that he'd been exposed to cholera.

"Go to your tent," he instructed.

Nate frowned. "Sir?"

"That boy is ill, and you've exposed yourself. Get to your tent and watch for stomach ailments."

Nate didn't argue, which was a mercy.

Grant clapped the young man's shoulder. "Go on now."

"Yes, sir."

As Grant slipped inside, relief filled every inch of him. Ginger lay next to her brother, her hand resting on his unbroken arm. He grinned at Buddy's unfettered arms and legs. Obviously Ginger had taken the liberty of removing his bindings.

Good! Grant couldn't even imagine the sort of pain that poor boy had endured. The position alone would have been excruciating. Nate was an idiot. Grant intended to discuss putting him on livestock detail instead of placing him as guard over anything.

Knowing that Ginger was safe was enough for Grant. He started to duck back outside, but a slight shiver tremored through her body. Even in sleep, she felt the cold. He took a horse blanket from the corner of the tent and opened it wide. Tentatively, he draped it across her body. As much as he tried not to, he couldn't help but note the soft curve of her hip as she lay on her side. Swallowing hard, he forced his gaze away from her figure and to her face. Then he caught his breath as he met her open eyes, flashing angrily.

She shot up to a sitting position. "What do you think you're doing?"

"Covering you up. You were shivering."

The anger left her face. "Oh."

"What are you doing in here?"

Once again, her eyes flashed. "I came to check on my brother, and it's a good thing I did. How dare you tie his hands and feet together?" Her bottom lip trembled. "You're supposed to help people. Instead, you hurt him." Grant had never seen her on the verge of tears.

"Don't you have anything to say for yourself?" Ginger demanded. "Well, I cut him loose, and no one is going to tie him up again. I wouldn't treat a buzzard that way, let alone a boy."

"I agree, Ginger," he said gently. "I'm not the one that tied him up. Nate did. And believe me, I just gave him a sound piece of my mind for doing it too. It won't happen again."

She stopped and her face contorted as it tried to match up her expressions with her rapidly changing emotions. But all she could muster was, "Oh."

"Toni was worried," he said, hunkering down so that he met her eye to eye where she sat, the blanket still covering the lower half of her body. "She came and woke me up to find you."

"I'm sorry. I didn't mean to worry her, but I had to spend more time with my brother. Make sure he wasn't afraid."

The words touched his heart. He'd rarely seen a tender side of Ginger, and yet this was the second time in one day that he'd witnessed it. "Why are you staring at me?" she asked, a frown creasing her brow.

"I just wondered how someone as ornery as you could be so nice to your brother."

"Insult me all you want," she said, folding her arms across her chest. "I'm not leaving Buddy. And as long as you force him to sleep in the supply tent, I'm sleeping out here with him. We're family, and we stick together."

"There's no earthly reason that I can think of that would make it a bad decision."

Her expression took a second to slide from haughty to surprised. "Really?" She smiled.

Grant found himself responding with a returning smile. "I think it would be fine. And probably a good idea to have someone looking out for him since you've already been exposed."

A yawn stretched her mouth. He didn't blame her for being exhausted. After all, here it was after midnight, and she had awakened early to the outlaw raid. She had to get up extra early in the morning for water detail, so he should let her get to bed.

"Since you're safe and sound, I suppose I'll go back to bed myself." He gave her a pointed look. "That is, after I let Toni know you're fine. You really shouldn't tell her you're going to take care of private business and then not come back for two hours."

Ginger's eyes widened. "I didn't think . . . I just assumed she'd be asleep. She could barely keep her eyes from closing when I left."

"She woke up and was worried sick about you. When you live in a group like this, you have to be considerate of other people."

"I am considerate! Don't I always get the firewood and always give Toni the best meat even before I take it to Miss Sadie to divvy up the rest?"

"You're good to Toni. No one would doubt that you love her like a sister."

"Okay, then . . ."

"For mercy sake," came a weak voice from the pallet.

"He's saying when you leave, let people know where you're going so they don't worry."

"Well, I'm not deaf, am I? I know what he said."

Grant took steps toward the pallet. Might as well take a look at the boy since he was awake. Scooting back to allow him room, Ginger stayed close enough that Grant felt her presence a little more acutely than he wished for. One thing was for sure: he didn't want to feel the feelings he had for Ginger. She was arrogant and rough, but something about her loyalty and softness showed a heart that could be touched. That part of her fascinated him and made him want to know her better.

"Are they keeping me locked up?"

Ginger's expression softened, and she captured Grant's gaze in a look that conveyed her worry. Obviously, the boy didn't realize how sick he was. Ginger took the cloth from the wash basin and wiped it across his glistening brow. "Of course you're not a prisoner. Once Blake sees you're not going to try anything, he'll let you go."

Ginger stood over Grant's shoulder blocking the light from the lantern hanging on the other side of the tent.

"Move back, Ginger," Grant said. The girl was absolutely hovering.

A quick examination showed the boy to be in the same condition as earlier that night. Stifling a yawn, Grant stood. "As far as his wounds go, I think he just needs to keep resting as much as possible. His body will heal. It'll just take some time." He looked down at Buddy. "How's the pain?"

"Bad, Doc."

Grant nodded. "I'll be right back with some laudanum. That should help. If nothing else, you'll sleep. But now, I want you to take some quinine. It'll fight the cholera."

Grant walked across the tent, keenly aware of Ginger's presence as she walked with him. "I want to talk to you," she said.

"Okay. Go ahead."

"Outside."

"Then let's go."

"Buddy," she said. "I'm going to have a talk with Grant. I'll be back."

He led Ginger away from the tent. Nate's brows scrunched together at the sight of Ginger. "How'd you get in there?"

Ginger scowled at him. "I tossed a few rocks, and you thought someone was walking and went to take a look."

That did it. Grant was definitely talking to Blake about that man. "Nate, go back to your position."

He led Ginger away from the tent. Out of earshot, he turned to her. "What can I do for you, Ginger?"

"Is Buddy really going to be fine?"

"I'm not God. I hope your brother will recover. Cholera is a scary disease."

She let out a breath, as lines appeared between her eyes. "What are we going to do if this spreads? Buddy will never forgive himself if he causes other folks to get sick."

"Let's just pray and hope for the best." He reached forward and rested his palm on her shoulder. "God is faithful. He knows what He's doing."

Ginger's face softened and she nodded. "I guess any God

that can help you turn a baby and save Little Sam can take care of my brother."

"God is sovereign, Ginger. We have to trust Him, even when His plans and actions don't seem to make sense to our human minds."

In a beat, her face hardened. "Don't tell me God would save one life and take another. Little Sam might be a baby, but my brother isn't much more than a child himself. You know he wants to be a doctor like you?"

"I didn't know. Hopefully he'll have that chance."

"I hope so, Grant. I just don't think I could bear to lose another brother." Her demeanor suddenly changed, and she shook off his hand. "Just make sure you try to save this one."

Before Grant could answer, the sound of Buddy's retching reached them. Ginger didn't wait to say goodbye, and Grant didn't blame her. She slipped quickly into the tent and Grant followed. As he helped hold Buddy over the pail, Grant thought back to her last words. "Just make sure you try to save this one." This one what? He made a mental note to question her about the comment. Because it sounded, for all he was worth, as though Ginger had just accused him of something.

Six

"I say we take those that ain't sick and move on."

Grant watched to see what Blake would do in this situation that was quickly becoming volatile. Barnabas Shewmate was typically an even-tempered young man, but his outburst spoke of fear—panic, even.

Blake stood on the flap of his wagon, standing tall enough so that all the folks that had attended the meeting could see and hear. He raised both hands for silence. "Now, listen up. We can't chance spreading this. We'll go ahead and travel three more days and push as hard as we can. But we'll be too close to Fort Boise to risk any travel after that until this thing runs its course."

"So we're sitting ducks for cholera or Indians or outlaws to just pick us off?" Barnabas yelled. "I'm taking my wife and leaving after tomorrow. The rest of you can stay behind." He glared at Blake. "You told us when we signed on with this outfit that we'd be in Oregon by now. If we wait any longer, we're going to be stuck in the mountains this winter. And I ain't chancing my family starving to death or worse."

"I'm goin' with Barnabas," Floyd Packer spoke up. "Listen, I don't want to cause trouble, but I say those of us that want to move on should do it now. If we wait another day, we might end up sick."

Grant moved forward and climbed onto the wagon next to Blake. "Listen, folks. If you've already contracted cholera, you won't know for a few more hours. Maybe a full day. Some of you have already come to me this morning complaining of stomach ailments. I can't confirm cholera in anyone yet, except the young man in the supply tent. But the fact is, if we all stay together, we can contain this thing."

"That's another thing I want to know," an older man spoke up. "Where'd that fella come from?"

"The scouts found him wounded in the woods."

"They shoulda left him in the woods, then."

"He's just a boy, people. We don't leave human beings to die in the woods."

Barnabas lifted his voice again. "Better him than us. I say we leave him and move on without him."

The sounds of panic rippled through the group. Grant couldn't help but be relieved that Ginger was off gathering water and couldn't hear this. He hated to think of what she'd have to say to these men. It wouldn't be good, and it certainly wouldn't help the situation any.

Blake raised his hands for silence, but it took a few minutes for people to calm down and pay attention. "We aren't the first wagon train to deal with cholera. Doc has a quinine regimen that should kill the disease if we get to it quickly enough. But if you leave, you'll be at the mercy of the sickness, without a doctor's care." He looked down at Floyd. "Do you want to risk your children's lives?"

The man averted his gaze.

"Now I suggest everyone get prepared. We'll cross the river today, and it's not going to be easy. Let's pack up. We'll leave within the hour."

Grant breathed a sigh of relief as the disgruntled group began to disperse. He turned to Blake. "Looks like we'll have to keep an eye on Shewmate. He could cause trouble."

Blake nodded, his lips pressed into a grim line. "How's the boy?"

"Worse. If he pulls through today, he'll likely live. Otherwise, we'll be burying him by morning."

"We'll keep him in prayer." Blake shook his head. "I just hope this doesn't spread."

Grant nodded. He, too, prayed Buddy would be the only case of cholera. But he knew that once the disease made an appearance, it usually didn't stop until it blazed a path of destruction lined with graves.

This river was the most challenging crossing so far. By the time the travelers made camp, they were only thanking God that no one had drowned. But it had been an exhausting day for Ginger, as she fought the oxen to get them across the busy water and worried about Buddy. She would have liked nothing better than to be part of the hunting detail. But Blake was sticking to his guns, and she was stuck on water detail.

Two filled pails of water hung from the yoke across Ginger's aching shoulders. "I'm nothing but a pack animal," she grumbled to Toni and Fannie, who also carried water for the camp.

"Stop complaining, Ginger," Toni chided. "We do this every single day, while you ride and hunt and do all the things you enjoy. It won't hurt you to do this for the time being. You know full well Grant will eventually talk Blake into putting you back with the scouts. So hush up and take your punishment like an adult instead of being so childish."

"Toni's right," Fannie said, her breathing coming in short bursts as she struggled under the weight of the yoke she carried. "You're mighty lucky Blake didn't order you out of the train. We're almost to Fort Boise, you know."

Ginger shrugged. "I'd have just followed the wagon train anyway. He'd eventually have let me just come back."

Fannie laughed. "You're probably right. Isn't she, Toni?"

Toni joined her in laughter.

"What's so funny about that?" She could hear the testiness in her voice, but mercy . . . why did they always laugh at her? They could show a little restraint, considering how worried she was about Buddy. It was touch and go right now. She ached to get finished with the water and go to him.

"Oh, Ginger. Don't be upset with us. It's just that Blake didn't want to let me and Toni join the wagon train either," Fannie said. "As a matter of fact, he downright refused us. We had to follow for a while before he spotted us. He gave in, but he wasn't too happy about it."

Ginger grinned as she grasped the irony.

"Seriously, though," Fannie said. "Don't push Blake too far, Ginger. He's a good man, but his good nature and adherence to my friendship with you will only go so far."

Ginger didn't want to put Fannie in a position to be at odds with Blake. She remembered fighting between her own parents and would never want to be the cause of Fannie and Blake arguing. "I'll be better from now on, but the thing I don't understand is why he never wants me to ride out from camp, but he doesn't mind if Two Feathers or Grant or any of the other scouts leave by themselves. I have to have a partner any time I want to ride away from camp. Even if it's not too far off. It doesn't seem fair to me. Especially when I could spot danger and take care of myself as well or better than any of the men, except maybe Sam and Blake."

"And Grant," Toni said.

"Well, I don't know about that."

Toni stopped beside a large rock and eased the yoke from her neck, careful not to spill any water. "I have to take a break."

"Thank goodness," Fannie said, following Toni's lead. "I was ready to stop ten minutes ago."

"Well, if you two are going to stop, I reckon I'd best do it, too." Secretly, she was also exhausted, but she'd rather die than admit her weakness.

Toni settled onto the rock and turned to Ginger. "I think it's only smart that you have to have a partner in order to leave camp. It's not like Blake gave the order just to confine you. He did it to keep you safe."

Ginger plopped down on the ground and stretched her legs. "I can take care of myself just fine. How does he think

I survived alone all those weeks before I met up with your wagon train at Fort Laramie?"

"That's not the point. Once you joined our wagon train, Blake became responsible for you."

Ginger rolled her eyes. "Blake Tanner isn't responsible for me. I am."

Toni gave a heavy sigh. "You're just being stubborn."

"I am not."

"You are too."

"Ladies," Fannie's voice interrupted. Concern filled Ginger at the weakness of Fannie's normally strong, sure voice.

Toni and Ginger exchanged a glance then turned toward their friend. "Are you okay?" Toni asked.

Panic widened Fannie's eyes and she shoved up from the rock and raced a few yards away before hunching over and retching.

"She's got the cholera!" Ginger said, hearing her fear.

"Ginger, hush," Toni whispered. She went to Fannie and rubbed her friend's back until she was spent. Toni dipped the edge of her apron in one of the buckets of water and wiped Fannie's face. "Does Blake know?" she asked softly.

Ginger frowned. "Does Blake know what? That she has the cholera?"

Fannie shook her head, ignoring Ginger completely. "I wanted to be sure first."

"Sure about *what?*"

Toni shot her a frown. "For heaven's sake, hush a minute. Fannie's in the family way."

Toni sounded so sure of herself, but Ginger wasn't convinced. She'd seen enough of this sort of thing—this sickness—over the last few hours that the thought of a baby just didn't seem likely.

"Well, how does she know it's not the cholera?"

"I've been sick like this for a week," Fannie said, sending her a wan smile. "Cholera would have already run its course whether I survived it or not."

Shocked into silence, Ginger watched her two friends as they sat next to each other on the rocks. Fannie's eyes glowed, and Toni's smile stretched across her whole face. For the life of her, Ginger couldn't see what in the world there was to be so happy about. Bringing a baby into the world when they still had two months of hard travel ahead, not to mention the real work beginning once they reached Oregon—it just didn't make sense.

"What in blazes was Blake thinking, letting this happen? You've barely been married any time at all."

She hadn't really meant to speak aloud, but now there was no taking it back. Guiltily, she slanted a glance at the two women. Fannie's glare demanded an explanation.

"Well . . . I mean, wouldn't it be smarter to wait until you get to your homestead and actually build a house for the little tyke to live in?"

"I didn't exactly plan for it to happen." Fannie's cheeks bloomed with color. "The Lord is in control of when a life leaves or enters the world."

"Fannie's right, Ginger." Toni gave a sigh and rolled her eyes at Ginger. "God doesn't typically follow our timing. And obviously He felt like a new baby for Blake and Fannie is a good thing, even if it's not the most convenient time."

"Maybe so," Ginger said. She pulled the yoke back onto her shoulders, sloshing water on the ground, which only added to her irritation. She shook her head at Fannie. "Maybe you should ask God to share the news with Blake, because I sure wouldn't want to be the one to do it."

"Ginger!" Toni planted her hands firmly on her hips. "That wasn't a very considerate thing to say."

"What? It's just the truth."

"No. It's the truth as you see it. Fannie is nervous enough as it is without you adding to her worry."

"It's okay, Toni," Fannie said glumly. "She's right. Blake's not going to be happy about this. Especially right now, when he's so worried about this cholera getting out of hand."

"Well, Blake knows where babies come from," Toni snapped in a way Ginger hadn't really seen before. "If he didn't want to chance a child coming in to the world, he shouldn't have taken his pleasure."

Ginger's face burned at Toni's candid speech. "If you're going to talk like that I'm going back to camp. Folk are likely waking up and ready for their water by now, anyways."

"We'll be there in a second."

Ginger hesitated. "Don't carry that," she said to Fannie. "I'll take mine to camp and be back for yours."

"Oh, no. I'll manage."

Toni placed a hand on Fannie's arm. "She's right. You can't carry water. You'll have to switch to a different chore. This one is too heavy for someone in your condition."

"I suppose you're right." Fannie's smile was weak as she looked at Ginger. "Thank you. I appreciate the offer."

Ginger warmed under the approving nod she received from Toni.

Still, she wouldn't want to be in Fannie's shoes. According to Toni, and even Grant, God had life firmly in his hand. But Ginger wasn't so sure. Buddy was growing weaker as the cholera raged through his body. Fear gripped Ginger at the very thought that her brother might not make it. He just had to. That was all there was to it. Was she really supposed to be alone in the world?

She had plans to make—plans to take Buddy and hightail it west where they could live the life Clem had always promised they'd have. Since he was gone, she would make it happen for her little brother. Clem would have wanted it this way. A smile tipped her lips at the thought. Yes, Clem would definitely have wanted her to take care of Buddy.

She'd been so wrapped up in her plot to avenge Clem's death that she hadn't even considered the need to get Buddy away from Web and the rest of the men. But she recognized the timing. She had to get her little brother away from here. Before Web did something stupid that involved her. Something she wouldn't be able to walk away from.

As soon as Buddy got well and strong again . . .

Grant noticed Ginger returning to camp, depositing her water buckets at Miss Sadie's campsite, and heading back out. Curiosity, combined with a realistic suspicion that she was going off from camp to be alone, forced him to follow her.

"Ginger!" he called out as they cleared the wagons. "Where do you think you're you going?"

She stopped short and turned to face him as he caught up to her. "To get water. This is my punishment, you know. Why aren't you taking care of my brother instead of bothering me?"

"Miss Sadie is sitting with Buddy for now. I'll help get him loaded into your wagon as soon as you get back from your chores." Ginger's brown eyes flashed in the early morning sun and her face softened. The smile disarmed him. "I'd appreciate that."

"My pleasure."

She took in his gaze for a few seconds before clearing her throat. "I best get back to my chores so we can get Buddy ready to go."

"Fine. I'm coming with you."

Exasperation moved across her features. "I have to finish up by myself."

"Why? You planning to run off again?"

Her jaw dropped. "And leave my brother?"

Grant realized that she would never do that. Still she was acting awfully strange. Even for Ginger. "I'm coming with you."

"Seriously, Grant." Her tone was beginning to sound desperate. "I don't want to hold you up. I'm just going after water. We're heading out in less than an hour. I'm sure you have plenty to do without playing nursemaid to me."

He pretended to consider her words, then he chuckled. "Nope. I can't think of anything."

A defeated scowl passed over her face. She let out a breath. "Oh, all right, fine then. Come with me. But don't ask any questions." She peered closer, fixing him with a look that told him how serious she was.

Now that made him all the more curious. "Fine. No questions."

Within a few minutes of silence, they came upon Fannie and Toni sitting on a boulder, their water buckets at their feet.

"Ginger! You brought Grant?"

"Against my will." Ginger scowled deeply. "I couldn't get rid of him." She walked straight to Fannie's water buckets and grunted as she pulled the yoke across her shoulders. "Sorry, Fannie. He refused to go away. I finally didn't have any choice but to bring him with me." She turned her face toward Grant and spoke with purpose. "But he's not allowed to ask any questions."

Fannie gave a weary smile. "It's all right."

Grant's instincts as a doctor kicked in as he searched Fannie's pale face. "You sick, Fannie?"

She nodded, her face blooming with color. "A little."

Grant walked across the rocky soil. He reached out and tested the temperature of her skin. "You're not feverish, but it's obvious you're not well. You'd better stay away from the water detail until we're sure you're not carrying cholera."

"I don't think this is cholera, I've been sick for a few days. This will most likely pass in a little while."

He assessed the situation: Ginger coming back for Fannie's buckets; the young bride ill, but sure it would pass in a little while; and finally, he wasn't allowed to ask questions.

"Oh . . ." he said.

Fannie, Ginger, and Toni all three glanced sharply at him.

"You're with child."

Ginger glared at him. "I thought I told you no questions."

"That, my girl," he said, taking the yoke from her, "was a statement of fact, not a question."

"What do you think you're doing?" Ginger demanded, making a grab for the water.

"Stop it. You're going to dump the buckets." Grant stepped back and slid the yoke across his own shoulders. "You've already carried water today. I'll take this one."

Taking a deep breath, Ginger apparently decided to give up. She tossed him a glare. "Thanks," she said through teeth clenched so tightly, it really didn't sound like a word at all. Grant grinned.

They walked in silence. When they reached the edge of camp, he turned to find her face was white as a boll of cotton. "Ginger. What's wrong? Are you hurt?"

"It's Web," she whispered. Grant set the water on the ground and took her arm. "What are you talking about? You're not making any sense. What about a spider's web?"

She gave a vehement shake of her head. "Not a spider's web. *Web*! The man talking with Blake." She nodded toward the wagon master who was, indeed, speaking with a stranger.

"Who is he?"

She turned her dread-filled gaze on him. "Grant," she whispered. "He's my pa, and I'm pretty sure he's got cholera, too."

Seven

Ginger would have chosen to be anywhere but sitting at Blake's camp, trying to decide how much truth to tell. Web would kill her if she ratted him out. Besides, to sell out Web would also be selling out Buddy and herself. And she couldn't do that to her brother. Blake stared at her, his eyes filled with accusation.

She swallowed hard. "I told you I saw my pa. I guess he got to worrying about Buddy and decided to look for him. It wouldn't take an experienced tracker much to figure out Buddy's here."

"And that's all there is to it? Your pa won't be making any trouble?"

Oh, she wanted to tell him to lock up any valuables and keep an eye on Web, but that information would dredge up all kinds of questions that she couldn't answer. Not yet anyway. Not until Buddy was safe, and she could take her brother and run away.

"I never speak for my pa, Blake. I'd like to assure you that he won't cause trouble, but if he does I'd be considered a liar and you'd think I betrayed you."

His eyebrows went up at her words. "I appreciate your honesty."

"The best I can say is keep an eye on him."

"I'll do that."

"Is that all?"

Blake nodded. "I'm going to ask you to do something."

Ginger waited, she wasn't used to people asking her anything. Especially the men in charge around here. "Yeah?"

"Keep an eye on your pa. I'm not asking you to spy on him and report back to me. But I think you've made enough friends in this wagon train that you wouldn't want any harm to come to anyone." He released a breath. "Grant doesn't think Web's got cholera. If he does, his symptoms aren't the same as other folks'. So I'm going to put him on water detail to take Fannie's place."

Ginger's emotions warred inside of her. In part, she felt pride that Blake trusted her. But it meant she had to put up with Web, and that didn't sit well with her.

But she had no choice. "I'll do my best."

"I know you will. You can go now."

Web had weaseled his way into the wagon train, pretending to be a loving pa, concerned for his wayward daughter and poor, ill son who had run off after his sister. It had been two full days of riding the trail hard, and all Ginger had wanted was to stay as far away from him as possible. If only Blake hadn't made that impossible.

Tempers were short, muscles ached, and the rocks were unforgiving. Sagebrush bit at the emigrant legs and annoyed the animals. Still, Blake pushed on with new fervor, allowing for no unnecessary stops and keeping the wagons rolling two hours past the time he normally did. He offered no apology and no explanation other than the obvious—that the train was already behind schedule and unless they pushed harder than they ever pushed, they'd be trapped by snow in the mountains and would likely all die before the spring thaw. The illness brought to the pioneers by Buddy had started to run its course. Buddy was still weak, but seemed better.

Darkness was setting in earlier these days, so not only did Ginger have to carry the yoke around her neck fetching water, but a lantern as well. Blake had ordered her to take Web along, so she could no longer avoid her pa.

It seemed that Blake felt like it might be providential, Web showing up the same day Fannie was forced off the water detail, so Web filled the slot immediately, much to Ginger's annoyance.

"I'm starting to see why you like these people," Web said. "They're the real salt of the earth. Sort of makes a man want to mend his ways and settle down into a respectable life."

But Ginger wasn't falling for it. So far, he'd remained silent about his reasons—his true ones—for joining the train, introducing himself as her and Buddy's pa, but Ginger knew what he was after. "You're right. They are good people, Web. You should remember that."

As though he hadn't heard a word she'd said, he glanced across the camp, staring at Fannie and Toni as they sat sharing coffee at Fannie's fire. "You're smart enough to make friends with the right folks anyway. I'm right proud of ya."

. "I don't know what you're talking about."

"Sure ya do. The wagon master's wife and the half-breed's sweetheart."

The way he said, "half-breed" set Ginger's teeth on edge. "Don't talk about Sam like that."

"Like whut?"

She looked at him askance.

Web's brow scrunched. "Ain't that what he is?"

Releasing a quick puff of air, Ginger shook her head in disgust. "He might be half-Sioux, but he's a good man and deserves respect."

"There ain't gonna ever come a day when I respect any breed."

Finally, his true self was showing up. It was about time. Now Ginger could start poking around for the truth. "What are you really doing here, Web?"

"I told you, I'm going straight. No more robbin'."

"I don't believe you." Part of her wished he was telling the truth, but every ounce of common sense told her otherwise. "What is it?"

His gaze narrowed. "What do you know about Mr. Harrison?"

Ginger gasped. "This is all about Mr. Harrison?"

Giving up all pretense, Web's hand shot out and gripped her forearm. "What do you know about the money?"

"Only that you're after it, if it exists."

"It exists. I saw that wagon master loading it for Harrison when they set out from that one-horse town of Hawkins, Kansas. Also noticed a false bottom on Harrison's wagon, so

I reckon he mighta moved the money box from the supply wagon to his own."

Ginger's jaw dropped with horror. "That's the real reason you didn't put up a fight about me going after the train, isn't it? You meant to follow it and rob these people anyway. You never cared about making anyone pay for Clem's death."

He beamed as though she'd been the one to come up with the idea in the first place. "You always was the smart one. Take after your ma that way. Be glad you don't take after her in other ways."

Ginger rolled her eyes. The last thing she needed was for him to start talking about the woman who had left him for another man so many years ago. "If you saw a money box, why did you wait so long to come after the train? You said three months. I figured you'd decided against coming after me."

"We had the law on us. Had to split up for a while. But when we met up a few weeks ago, I said, 'Fellas, how about we go after that wagon train? And I bet we'll find my little girl close by.' 'Course, I never thought you'd've joined up with them like you done."

"I told you," she said keeping her voice low. "I didn't join up with anyone. But I like the idea of settling in Oregon."

He sent her a fierce scowl. "What would a lone girl do in Oregon?"

She shrugged because this was the first time she'd truly considered the possibility. "File a claim."

Web threw back his head and laugh from his belly. "You mean to tell me you think you're going to become a farmer?

Get it out of your head, gal. I told you already, I'm gonna be needin' a female for the next plan I got in mind."

Ginger's stomach churned at the implication that she would have no choice but to leave the wagon train folks and rejoin Web.

"The thing I have most in my head right now is Buddy being so sick, Web. I'm worried about him."

Web's head nodded grimly. "He's bad off. That's the truth."

"What about you, Web? You seemed so sick that first day. What happened?"

He gave a laugh. "I'm too wicked to be sick for long."

He was wicked, that was for sure, but Ginger knew better than to attribute his health to that fact. "Be serious, Web."

He shrugged. "I don't know. Sometimes I feel sick, and other times I don't."

"Miss Sadie has had cholera before, and Grant says that makes her not likely to get it again. Have you ever had it?"

"No."

Footsteps crunched over the dried leaves on the ground, and Web and Ginger turned to find Elijah headed toward them through the brush.

Web practically growled at the newcomer. "What are you doin' away from camp, Elijah?"

"I came to tell you that Murray died this morning. And three more of the men have come down with cholera." His eyes scrutinized Web. "I can see you've come through it without much illness at all, but it's sweeping through your men back at camp."

The way Elijah eyed Web, Ginger wondered for the first

time if maybe her pa had been faking it all along or if Elijah suspected it anyway.

"What do you expect me to do about it?"

"Web!" Ginger said. "You're their leader. If they're afraid, they need you."

Elijah nodded his approval. "Your daughter is right. The men are afraid. Some are talking about leaving."

Web shrugged his meaty shoulders. "I don't force no one to stay."

Except for me, Ginger thought ruefully. Besides, if the men dispersed, they could spread cholera across the entire territory. "Web, the men could end up at one of the forts or any number of friendly Indian villages. Not to mention the wagon trains."

"Well, that's their choice, ain't it?"

Elijah caught Ginger's gaze, and it seemed as though his frown was more of concern than anger. For an outlaw, he did seem to have some scruples. "That's not the point," he said. "Ginger is saying, plainly, the men could end up spreading out in all directions. They could infect hundreds of people. They need your leadership to get them to stay put. I'm starting to feel sick, myself. If I have it, I won't be able to help very much longer."

"Well, that's too bad. I got other things to do."

Ginger turned to Elijah. "What they need is a doctor. Do you have any quinine in camp?"

"Not that I know of."

"All right. I can try to get some. But I don't know if Grant will part with any. He's worried about the wagon train."

Elijah nodded. "And a sorry band of outlaws isn't likely to be on his list of priorities."

"I don't think so," Ginger said. "But he's a good man; he might share some if he realizes how fast it's spreading."

Web reached out in a flash and grabbed Ginger's arm, his fingers biting into the tender flesh. "What do you mean he's a good man? Lane was right. You have gone soft."

Ginger pulled away, emboldened for some reason, by Elijah's presence. "Maybe I have gone soft in a lot of ways. I don't know what I think anymore. But no matter what he did back then, he's a good doctor now. You should have seen the way he saved Yellow Bird's baby. If anyone will get us through the cholera, it'll be him."

Elijah nodded. "It's good to know he's so competent. Hopefully he's compassionate, as well."

"Come back tomorrow and I'll try to have some quinine for you."

Elijah shook his head. "If I wait until tomorrow, half the men will be gone or dead. We need something tonight to give them hope."

Ginger's heart raced at the thought of having to approach Grant. The other alternative was to steal the quinine, but she didn't feel right about that.

"We have to get this water back to camp. I'll find Grant and try to convince him to help. Meet me back here in an hour."

"Thank you," Elijah said. His gaze rested on her for a second. "I overheard your conversation with Web. If you want to go to Oregon, you should."

"Mind your own business," Web growled. "I didn't raise my daughter to be some farmer."

"Farming is a respectable profession, Web. It seems to me that a man would want his children to find something better than he has himself. Especially if that means she isn't a thief and a liar."

Ginger's heart lifted to hear Elijah's words. Not that it would do any good as far as Web was concerned. But it was nice to hear someone support her.

"I'll be back here in an hour with an answer," she said.

Elijah nodded. "I'm obliged."

"Don't thank me yet. I might not be able to convince Grant."

He turned and disappeared into the shadows as quickly as he'd appeared. Ginger turned to Web. "One thing he said is right, Web."

"You takin' his side, gal?"

"No. I said there's one thing he's right about."

"What's that?"

"The fact is that it's not good for you to be away from the men right now. They need you. Once this is all over, they won't have any confidence in you."

"You worry too much." He grinned. "Once I come back with Harrison's money, I guarantee you no one will think Lane should be leading them yet. Who knows?" He sent her a wink. "Maybe they'll all die, and you and I won't have to share with them."

Ginger wasn't sure whether he was joking or not, but horror filled her chest, just the same. "Web. That's just not right. Those men have followed you for a long time, most of them, you can't possibly wish them to die."

He rolled his eyes. "I knew it. You're going soft."

"Think whatever you want, but you can't steal Mr. Harrison's money. He just lost his wife in a twister a few months ago. It's not right."

Web shoved his finger in Ginger's face. "I'll decide what's right and what ain't. Don't forget I been taking care of you since you was born. Have I ever done wrong by you, yet?"

Was he serious? He didn't consider raising her in a band of thugs and thieves to be slightly wrong? It was no use. She could talk until she was blue in the face and he'd never see reason. Web was just too old and set in his ways.

"Let's get the water and head back to camp," she said.

He grabbed hold of her arm. "Don't you think about double-crossing me, girl."

"What are you talking about?"

"You know. Yer different now. Like one of them. But don't forget who your family is. That's all I'm sayin'. Those people would toss you out in the desert all alone if they got wind of what you really are. And wouldn't that be a real shame if they found out?"

The veiled threat in his eyes made her heart race. "I don't plan to double-cross anyone."

He nodded and let her go. "Keep it that way."

Ginger picked up her buckets and headed toward the water. It hadn't occurred to her to go against Web. This was what they did. Stealing to live. She didn't have to like it, but she couldn't go against her own flesh and blood.

Guilt squeezed her heart as she was pulled between loyalty to Web and the wagon train folks. For the first time that she could remember, she truly understood what was decent and right, and she didn't like being on the other side of the issue.

Web had been right. She was different now. It felt funny. Not good. Suddenly, pulled between her old life and the future she craved in Oregon, Ginger honestly didn't know where she belonged.

Ginger went straight to the supply tent when she returned to camp carrying the water. She slipped inside to find Grant there with Buddy.

"How is he?" she asked, setting the buckets on the floor and stepping forward. His chest rose and fell steadily, and he seemed to be resting more peacefully than he had for two days. "He's better?"

Grant nodded. "He's lucky. He'll be a little weak for a few days, but I had hope when he didn't die yesterday that he'd pull through."

"You never said anything."

Grant stood and offered her his seat next to the pallet. "I didn't want to get your hopes up, just in case I was wrong."

Ginger looked down at Buddy. His pale face was sunken, and he looked ten years older than he had three days ago. "Are you sure he's getting better?"

Grant rested a warm hand on her shoulder. "Yes. He's over the worst. He hasn't been sick in several hours, and he's kept water down. So it's a real encouraging sign."

"Thank you, Grant."

Turning, she took a breath and faced him. "I have a favor to ask."

He squatted down eyelevel with her. "You looked troubled. What can I do?"

"I need some of the supply of quinine."

He frowned. "What do you mean? Are you ailing?"

"Oh, no. It's not me. It's just. . ."

How could she tell him that she needed part of his precious supply of medicine to treat the very men responsible for bringing the disease to the wagon train in the first place?

"The outlaws?"

Ginger's eyes went wide. "How did you know?"

He gave her a rueful smile. "You know, it doesn't take much to figure out that your pa and Buddy came at the same time as the outlaws raided. Sam and Blake aren't fooled. They've also been keeping an eye on the tracks the outlaws have been making. They don't seem too worried about hiding. If I was trying to hide out, I'd be inclined to make my camp a little farther away than they have."

Ginger gave a nod. "I agree. I don't know what Web was thinking."

"Well, at any rate, now you know why Blake has doubled the sentries."

"What do Sam and Blake intend to do?"

"I'm not sure. I imagine they'll contact the law or turn them over to the soldiers once we get to Fort Boise."

Panic washed over her. "Buddy hasn't done anything, Grant. All he's ever wanted was to be a doctor like you. I understand turning in the rest of them. Me, even. But not Buddy."

"It's not my call." He gathered a breath. "I can't spare the quinine, Ginger. Three more cases are confirmed this morning. I'm most likely going to run out before I can administer it to the rest of our sick folk." His eyes clouded with regret. "I'm sorry. I wish there was more I could do."

Ginger rose slowly as disappointment and anger built inside of her and bubbled over. "You're sorry? Men will die, and you're sorry? They may be nothing more than worthless outlaws to you, Grant Kelley, but I was raised with those men. They're like brothers. Some of them, anyway."

"I'm sorry. Truly I am. I wish there was something . . ."

"Save your *sorry*s for someone who believes you," she spat. "I can't believe I almost changed my mind about you."

"Here, now. Just a minute. You're not being fair. My first responsibility is to these people. I'm sorry that disappoints you, but I can't apologize for not taking our small amount of medicine and giving it away to thieves and cutthroats."

"Like I said," she hissed standing over him, "save your apologies for someone whose brother you didn't kill."

She stormed out of the tent, fighting hard against tears of anger. Oh no. She wouldn't give into them. Grant Kelley wasn't worth one single tear.

Eight

Grant frowned after Ginger as the stubborn, infuriating woman slammed out of the tent, sloshing water from her buckets as she left. What did she expect him to do? Let the wagon train folks die off one by one so those confounded outlaws could recover to rob another day? So they could kill another man's wife? She was being completely unreasonable. But then, when had she ever shown a lick of reason?

Buddy moaned a little and opened his eyes. "Water . . ." he mumbled.

Grant dipped the tin cup into the water bucket and brought it to the boy's lips. "Take it easy," he said as Buddy drank with greed.

"Thank you," he said and rested back on his pillow as though the very act of lifting his shoulders long enough to take a sip was too much for him.

"You're welcome, son." Grant patted Buddy's shoulder. "You're going to be fine, now."

Buddy nodded. "I knew it. I heard Ginger praying for me the other night. I knew right then that I was going to get well."

Surprise lifted Grant's brow. "I didn't know Ginger was the sort of woman who prays."

"She never was before. I think somethin's changed her, being with this wagon train. She's nicer than she used to be. Don't frown near as much." His eyes were closed again.

Grant digested this information in silence. She didn't frown as much as she used to? Then she must have been one perpetual growl before she joined the wagon train. He'd never seen such a grumpy woman.

"I heard what you said about the rest of the group," Buddy said, his speech coming more slowly, quieter. "Ginger's just thinking of Clem, that's all."

"What do you mean?"

"Our brother . . ." The boy faded and Grant knew that no more answers were forthcoming.

He gathered up his supplies and left the tent, coming face to face with Miss Sadie. The woman had worked around the clock as new cases were popping up all over camp. She worked every bit as hard as he did, and Grant honestly didn't know what he would have done without her.

"Two more cases," she said grimly, not wasting time on greetings and niceties. She shook her head. "This is bad. We have to stop the spread before we lose half our people."

"I know, Miss Sadie, but I don't see how."

"We should make sure those men stay out of camp from now on, for one thing," she said with a huff.

"You know about them?"

Miss Sadie nodded. "Only a fool wouldn't put two and two together."

"Ginger asked me for quinine to give to those outlaws," he said, the words bitter in his mouth. "How could she even ask me to risk running out when our own people are in the middle of this epidemic?"

"Those are her people."

"Her people."

"Don't sound so angry. A person doesn't choose where they come from."

"She doesn't have to want to doctor them, does she? She knows they are no good."

"No good?" Miss Sadie shook her head. "Who are you to decide who is or isn't good?"

People were beginning to stare. Grant dropped his tone and leaned in. "They're outlaws."

"And every bit as precious in God's sight as anyone one of us. From you and me, to Yellow Bird's newborn babe."

Grant's thoughts returned to an awful, nightmarish day seven years ago when men just like these attacked the stagecoach where he and his wife rode. Sarah had just told him she was pregnant the week before so the entire ride until the attack had been filled with excitement and discussion about baby names, supplies, the blanket she was knitting as they rode along. When he had found that partial blanket later, it was soaked in Sarah's blood.

"Maybe, but I'm not risking the lives of one of these good, decent folks for the likes of those vermin." He couldn't discuss it anymore. "If you'll excuse me, Miss Sadie, I'd best go and check on Edna Stewart."

Miss Sadie nodded and patted him on the shoulder.

"You're a good, godly man, Grant. Don't let bitterness make you forget that."

Grant nodded, squeezing the older woman's hand as he walked past. He drew a deep breath. There had to be a lesson in this somewhere. He just wasn't sure what. Ginger would surely see reason and realize he couldn't give up the wagon train's supply of medicine. It wouldn't matter who needed it. They came first, and there was precious little quinine, as it was.

He only hoped there would be enough to get them through the worst of the epidemic.

Ginger dreaded having to face Elijah. How could she tell him that there was no help to be had. She knew she owed Grant an apology, too. Only an unreasonable fool would hold a grudge against a man trying to save an entire wagon train of folks.

That, however, didn't make her task any easier. Heavy-hearted, she trudged up the ridge to her meeting place with Elijah. She found a boulder and sat to wait for him. Her thoughts went to the group of dying men in the camp. They didn't deserve to die without at least someone trying to save them. But it was too late for Murray. James would be next, then who? Yuley? Poor, slow, Yuley, who barely knew his own name half the time. He'd never understand being so sick.

Tears formed in Ginger's eyes. Sure, these men might be thieves, but they weren't all bad. No matter what anyone thought. They didn't deserve to die off, one by one, without anyone caring for them.

Dead leaves crackled, and she turned, expecting to find Elijah. Surprise lifted her brow at the sight of Miss Sadie coming toward her carrying a burlap bag.

"Miss Sadie? What are you doing out here?"

She shoved the bag toward Ginger. "Onions. Boil them good and feed the broth to anyone complaining of cholera symptoms."

"Onions?"

Miss Sadie nodded. "Nature's the best cure for most ails. I learned about this from an old midwife back home. But too late to save my family. It'll kill the disease from the inside out if you get to it fast enough."

"Why are you telling me about this? Grant's the one you ought to be talking to. He's so all fired sure the quinine is going to run out. He'll be overjoyed with another form of treatment."

"You sound about as mad as a wet hen. Something you want to talk about?"

"No," Ginger said flatly. There was nothing to say on the subject. And if she started spouting her opinion of doctor Grant Kelley, she'd likely say too much.

"Well, don't talk about it then, but I had a talk with Grant," Miss Sadie said frankly. "He told me you asked for quinine."

"Yes, and he turned me down flat."

"As he should have."

"You too, huh?"

The older woman's eyes narrowed. "What's that supposed to mean?"

"So much for Christian charity when it comes to out-laws." She sniffed her disdain at the hypocrisy.

"Now, you listen up young lady," Miss Sadie said, de-manding Ginger's gaze, unyielding in her determined stance. "Christian charity doesn't mean giving away our small supply of medicine and letting a wagon train full of children die. And if you think it does, then you have a mighty confused idea of what being a Christian is."

"Maybe I do. But Grant does too, if you ask me."

"Well, I didn't ask you, and it just so happens that the reason I brought the onions was so you can take them to your outlaw friends."

Ginger gave a gasp. "They aren't my friends."

"Well, I'm not going to belabor the coincidence of the outlaw attack happening just before your brother and pa showed up. And lo and behold, now there's a camp of no-goods needing your help. What a string of coincidences, indeed." Miss Sadie rolled her eyes.

Well, when she put it that way, there was no point in de-nying anything. But did she have to be so sarcastic about it? Ginger's cheeks burned, but she refused to give in to the em-barrassment. She lifted her chin and forced herself to look Miss Sadie straight in the eye.

"Have you told Grant about the onions?" she asked. "Maybe he'd be a little more charitable if he knew there might be another remedy after the quinine runs out."

Miss Sadie shook her head. "I haven't had a chance to talk to him yet. Once I recalled the concoction, I got Yellow Bird making a strong batch back at our camp, and then I came to find you before you sent your outlaw friend away empty-handed."

The woman was as stubborn-minded as an old worn out mule. "I told you they are not . . ."

Miss Sadie held up a weathered hand in silence. "And I thought I told you I'd not argue the point."

"Well, they're not my friends," Ginger muttered.

Without acknowledging her words, Miss Sadie continued. "We'll need to round up all the onions we can find and trust God that there will be enough."

"You think we could run out of those too?"

Miss Sadie's shoulders rose and fell. "That's up to God, I suppose."

"What about Fort Boise? It's only a day's ride on horseback. I bet they're loaded down with onions, wild and planted."

Miss Sadie shook her head. "We can't risk passing along the cholera to the folks for the fort. Besides, two families have left the wagon train, I'm sure word will reach the fort soon, and they'd turn us away, anyhow." She nodded at the bag in Ginger's hand. "You just do your best to make those last. Feed the most of the broth to the sickest and be sure to give it to even the strongest at the first sign of sickness. That'll hopefully keep the disease from getting out of hand in the ones who aren't sick yet."

Still stinging from Grant's rejection, Ginger gave a bitter scowl. "You sure you want to part with these for a bunch of outlaws?"

"Would I have brought them to you otherwise?"

"I guess not." Remembering the worry clouding Grant's

eyes, Ginger gave a resigned little sigh. "I'm sure Grant will be relieved for now. According to him, the quinine won't last long if he can't get the disease under control soon."

Miss Sadie smiled and dropped to the boulder next to Ginger. "That's the problem with educated doctors."

A frown creased Ginger's brow and she peered closer at Miss Sadie. "What's that supposed to mean?"

A shrug lifted the woman's shoulders. "They think they have more control over these things than God." Ginger squinted against the midafternoon's glow as the sun glared through snow-frosted trees.

"Doesn't God help those that help themselves?"

"He is also sovereign, my dear. And whether this thing stops with only a few victims or wipes out the entire wagon train is up to Him."

"Then why bother trying to save anyone?"

Miss Sadie gave a weary smile. "Because it's not in our nature to sit back and not try."

A branch crackled behind them and both women turned. Elijah, pale and trembling, stood in the distance. Ginger's heart clenched.

"I reckon this fellow is looking for you?" Miss Sadie asked.

Ginger nodded. "He's the one I'm supposed to meet about the medicine."

Elijah took a step forward and crashed to the ground in a dead faint.

"He's not going to make it back to his men alone."

"Blake'll never agree to bringing him to camp."

Miss Sadie gave a grim nod. "You're right about that."

"What are we going to do?"

"We'll just have to go to that camp and nurse those men."

"What are you talking about? You want to ride into a camp of outlaws?"

"We can't leave them to die."

If cholera had swept through the entire group of men, she had no choice but to try to save the ones that could still be saved.

Her mind began to spin. "All right. If Yellow Bird and Toni will agree to bunk together in Toni's wagon, you and I could load Elijah into your wagon and take him back to his camp."

Miss Sadie nodded. "Exactly what I was thinking." She gave Elijah a compassionate glance, then turned to Ginger. "You stay here, and I'll go back to camp and make all the arrangements."

"Think Blake'll give you any trouble?"

"It's not so much Blake I'm worried about."

"Oh? You know how he feels about me going off away from the wagon train."

Miss Sadie gave her a pat on the arm and snatched the hem of her dress up from the ground as she prepared to leave. "Grant is the one who's likely to pitch a fit over you leaving camp this time."

"Grant?" Ginger couldn't hold back the bewildered frown. "Why would he? He won't even let me around the sick folks. Even though he knows I'd have likely got sick by now if I was going to."

"Mark my words, the good doctor is going to have plenty to say about your leaving camp to go off nursing a bunch of outlaws. Like I said, if I was a betting woman, I'd wager he'll likely be the one crying in the wilderness over this."

Ginger gave a sniff, ignoring the way her heart leapt at the suggestion. "I wouldn't wager on that one, Miss Sadie. You'd lose your shirt for sure. Trust me, he'll be as glad to be rid of me as I am to get away from him."

"*If* I were a woman given to gambling, I might have to make that wager, my girl. And believe me, I'd win. I've seen the way that man looks at you. And I happen to know he's not going to be glad to see you go."

Ginger very much doubted that, but why bother arguing with Miss Sadie?

Elijah groaned. His brow glistened with sweat. Ginger gave his skin a light touch. "He's awfully hot, Miss Sadie."

Miss Sadie nodded. "I'll be back soon. Here." She gave her apron a firm grip and tore off a square the size of a hanky. "Dip this in the water bucket and wipe down his face to try to cool him off."

Ginger took the cloth and knelt beside the man. He seemed a nice enough sort. She had to wonder why he had hooked up with the riffraff in Web's band of outlaws. He moaned again and his eyes opened, glassy and barely focusing.

"Take it easy, Elijah," she said, trying to keep her tone as soothing as possible when a stick was poking into her shin and causing no end of irritation. "We're going to take care of everything."

With a strength she never would have guessed he had, he grabbed her wrist.

"Hey!" she hollered and yanked it away, jumping to her feet. "Try that again and I'll leave you here to fend off the wolves. How would you like that in your condition?"

"Ginger," he said in a voice barely above a whisper. "I have to tell you . . ."

"You don't have to tell me anything except you're sorry for grabbing me and scaring me half to death."

Scaring her? Web was right—she was going soft. Six months ago, she'd have fought a man for calling her scared, now she was admitting it to a stranger?

"Your brother . . ."

"What's Buddy got to do with this? You better leave him alone."

He shook his head vehemently but didn't utter another word. The retching began and continued until he fainted, exhausted and spent.

Ginger tried not to be sick herself as she took the cloth and cleaned him up as best as she could. As she sat waiting for Miss Sadie to return, she wondered, could she really nurse five or six men just like this?

Nine

Grant couldn't believe what he was hearing. The fact that Blake had even considered such a cockeyed suggestion let alone gave his approval was downright idiotic. The whole notion made Grant wonder if the wagon master was ailing himself.

"That's ridiculous!" he heard himself utter. "Ginger has no business going into that group of cutthroats and debasing herself."

"She grew up with those men," Miss Sadie said with quiet amusement written all over her face. "Besides, I'll be there, too."

Grant snatched onto this forgotten slice of information. "That's another thing," he said, stepping closer to Blake, "What are we going to do without Miss Sadie? I need her help nursing these people."

Blake leveled a gaze at him. "Didn't I see Buddy Freeman helping you?"

"That boy is so weak he could barely carry a ladle of water, let alone a bucket. He isn't much help."

"So you carry the bucket," Miss Sadie said with her "my mind's made up" tone of voice. "Let him carry the quinine. There's not much else you can do for the sick, anyway. You'll be fine with the boy's help. I'm needed elsewhere." She peered closer and her gray eyebrows rose. "Unless *you'd* like to go help Ginger?"

Grant was just about to take her up on the offer when Blake cleared his throat. "Hold on now. We can't be sending our only doctor off on a mission to help another camp when we got our own sick."

Grant sent him a scowl. "You're right, I guess. But I'm telling you, this isn't a good idea. If Ginger has been trying to run away from these fellows, why are we just letting her go back in?"

Miss Sadie put her hands on her hips. "First of all, did Ginger ever say she was trying to run away from them?"

Grant stared down at the ground, racking his brain. "Well, no, but then she never admitted she was even part of that group, either." Grant fingered the hat he held in his hands. "At least not until I point-blank told her we'd figured it out."

"Well, obviously she feels she needs to go. Personally," Blake said, "I find that reassuring. I was beginning to wonder if the girl had any scruples about her at all."

Grant's ire rose, and he shot a glance to the wagon master. "That girl has more loyalty to friends and sense of integrity than just about anyone I know."

Blake's lips twitched. "How do you figure?"

But before Grant could mention her dedication to her friends and brother and how she always brought extra food in for families with a passel of youngsters to feed or older folks, Blake continued, "Because I'm talking about the girl that won't take orders, lied about her brother and the outlaws, and then lied again about her pa."

Well, shoot. He had a point there.

Miss Sadie stepped in. "This ain't getting us anywhere. The fact is, Blake's already given his permission. Ginger and I will go to the outlaw's camp and do our best to keep them alive."

"Long enough to hang," Grant muttered.

Blake expelled a frustrated breath. "You seem to forget that loyal, sweet girl you're so worried about is one of them."

"I never said she was sweet." Grant shoved his hat back onto his head. "Besides, it's not her fault she was born to that Web character, and I'm still not convinced she didn't run away and join us for a better life."

"She joined us because Sam paid her to look after Toni."

Thunder and lightning, he was right. "Maybe so, but she was still apart from them and that tells me all I need to know until someone proves otherwise."

Miss Sadie chuckled.

Grant turned on her. "What's so funny?"

She shrugged and continued to grin broadly. "Nothing much. Except if I was a bettin' woman, I'd be jangling a few extra coins right now."

Without awaiting a response, she gave him an affectionate pat on the arm as she walked past. "I best round up my things and get going back to Ginger. Yellow Bird ought to have her things moved by now."

Frustration welled inside Grant's breast. He wasn't ready for the situation to be settled. Not if it meant he'd lost the fight.

There was so much he still wanted to argue. And he wasn't even sure why. All he knew was that the thought of Ginger bending over those men and ministering to them brought out every protective instinct he thought long gone. Feelings he'd thought died with his Sarah. He didn't like the picture in his mind at all. What if she got to that camp and the men weren't even sick? What if it had all been some kind of trick to get her back there? That would mean she and Miss Sadie both would be in trouble.

He turned and opened his mouth to say as much to Blake, but the wagon master held up his hand. "I don't like us being on the opposite side of the fence, my friend, but I've already said my piece. We have no choice but to try to get this thing under control as soon as possible. That means the outlaws have to get treated, too. And even if it isn't just about containing the cholera, we can't call ourselves God-fearing if we leave them to die without any kind of medicine."

Grant gave a snort. "Onions aren't exactly medicine."

"The Indians have been using plants to cure all kinds of ills for longer than either of us has been alive, so if Miss Sadie says she thinks this onion remedy will work, I'm inclined to believe her."

"Fine, put your faith in plants instead of medicine. Why not invite a Cheyenne medicine man to do a dance?"

Blake rolled his eyes. "I got better things to do than argue with you about this."

"I have better things to do, as well." He took a short breath. "I'm telling you, Blake. This feels wrong."

"It feels right to me."

"Well, maybe it wouldn't if it was . . ." Grant drew in the words before he could finish the sentence. Blake's eyes showed interest as he waited.

"If it was what?"

Shaking his head, to clear it more than anything, Grant expelled the breath he'd just sucked in. "Nothing," he shot back.

Blake looked as though he might pursue the issue, but a pale, shaking Barnabas Shewmate ran into Blake's camp area. "You gotta come, Doc," he said. "It's my Jenny. She's bad off."

"I'm coming, Barnabas. I have to go to my tent first. I'll need my bag."

"No, you got to come now!"

Grant took the young man by the shoulders and looked deeply into his eyes. "Listen. I can't help Jenny unless I go and get my medicine. I'll be there directly. I give my word. Go sit with her and hold her hand until I get there."

Fannie came out of the tent. "I'll go to Jenny," she said. "You stay with Grant."

"No, Fannie," Blake's voice was firm. "Get back inside."

"Blake, if it's God's will for me to have this baby, I will. I can't stay hidden away when there are so many who need help. I've already been around enough of the illness. If it's going to take hold, it will."

Blake shot a gaze at Grant, an appeal for support. "Fannie, there's no need to tire yourself out. I'll be at the Shewmates' tent in a few minutes."

"How much do you think Barnabas will be able to reassure her? He's as skittish as a newborn colt."

Grant nodded.

"She's about to deliver their first baby, Grant," Fannie pressed. "She'll need another woman there. And who more reassuring than the wagon master's wife?" She turned to Blake. "I'm going."

"Fannie . . ." he said, warning in his tone.

She scowled. "We agreed from the start of our marriage that you wouldn't try to bully me. I know you're concerned. But there's nothing I could do that would hurt this baby by going and sitting next to a sick, scared woman."

"A woman sick with the deadliest disease I've ever seen. Fannie, I've seen it wipe out wagon trains before."

"Then sitting next to Jenny Shewmate and holding her hand isn't going to make much difference."

Barnabas let out an impatient groan. "Doctor, please. She's in an awful lot of agony."

Wrapping her shawl around her slim body with purpose, Fannie walked to her husband, rose onto her tiptoes, and brushed a quick kiss to his lips. "I'll be back later."

"One hour." He gripped her shoulders and held her fast as he looked deeply into her eyes. "If you're not back in one hour, I'll come and carry you back to me. Clear?"

Her lips curved into the softest of smiles. "Clear."

And just like that, she was gone, leaving Grant mesmerized by the loving exchange.

Barnabas grabbed his arm, pulling him from the stupor. "Let's go, Doc."

"She's as likely to make it out of this as anyone on the wagon train, Blake." Not that it was any consolation. Just a fact.

Blake scowled. "Or just as likely to die."

The wheels were set into motion now and only God decided when the dying would stop and the healing begin. Blake captured his gaze as each man caught the full brunt of the exchange. "I shouldn't have let her go," Blake said, his eyes piercing and full of regret. And all at once, Grant wasn't sure if he meant Fannie or Ginger. Either way, he answered for Ginger's sake. "She knew what she had to do."

Blake nodded. There was nothing more for either of them to say. Jenny Shewmate was near delivery. Would she deliver a baby stricken with cholera? Would she even live that long?

Please God, he silently prayed, *work a cure before any more of these good people die.*

Ginger scowled as they entered the filthy, foul-smelling camp. Next to her on the wagon seat, Miss Sadie shook her head, her own disgust showing on her wrinkled, leathery face.

Relief flowed through her as Yuley greeted her with a weak wave. Yuley was just plain good. He was too simple-minded to form a thought on his own and just did as he was told. The one decent thing Web had ever done was keep Yuley on after his brother died, even though the man was more trouble than he was worth, according to Web. She smiled and waved back. "Good to see you're on your feet, Yuley," she called.

Trembling and visibly ill, he nevertheless managed to make his way to the wagon. "It's mighty fine to see you, Missy Ginger. You ain't sick, are you?"

Ginger hopped down and offered Miss Sadie a hand from the wagon. "No, Yuley. And I'm here to help you get better."

"I'd be obliged, Missy." He turned to Miss Sadie. "Can I take your bag for you, ma'am?" Ginger had to wonder where Yuley had learned his manners. It certainly wasn't from anyone in that camp.

Miss Sadie's gruff exterior melted beneath the young man's innocent desire to be a gentleman. "I think I best hang onto this while you go set yourself down and wait for us to fix you up some medicine. Okay?"

He frowned, obviously troubled at the suggestion. Ginger stepped in. She slung a maternal arm around his shoulders, nearly gagging at the stench of his unwashed body. "It's okay, Yuley. Miss Sadie might be old, but she's stout. You don't seem quite as sick as some of those men on the bedrolls, so we want you to save your strength and get well fast. We'll need your help, but first, we have to get you well." She patted his back, then moved upwind.

A flicker of understanding lit his eyes. "Okay, Miss Ginger." He shuffled off toward the pit that barely had enough coals still burning to be considered a fire.

Another man sat by the stone circle, as well. Ginger peered closer to confirm it was a grizzled older man by the name of Dale Thane. As far as outlaws went, Dale was one of the better ones. Until he was crossed, anyway. Ginger had seen him bite a man's ear off in a fight over a lost pair of gloves. He was old but wiry, and most of the men knew not to cross him. Especially if he'd had whiskey.

"How you holding up, Dale?" she called out.

"Better than them fellas," he called with a sweep of his arm.

Four or five more men lay on bedrolls around the camp. In the dusky evening, Ginger couldn't tell if any of them were breathing or not. And she had to wonder where the rest of the band was. There should have been close to fifteen men in the group. Surely they weren't all dead. "Where's Lane and the rest of the men?"

"Gone. Most of 'em left a couple days ago. Lane left this mornin', early."

"So much for honor among thieves," Miss Sadie muttered.

Ginger moved around to the back of the wagon and let down the gate. She shook Elijah's foot gently. "We're going to need you to wake up and help us get you settled."

Weak, white, and shaking so hard he could barely move, Elijah sat up. Ginger climbed into the back of the wagon and let him hang onto her while he somehow found the strength to pull himself to the edge of the wagon. He stopped a moment for a breather as his legs dangled off the side. "I'm sorry I'm not more help."

"Hogwash," Miss Sadie said, sliding up under his arm as Ginger did the same on the other side.

Looking around, Ginger couldn't find a lick of firewood. She gave a snort. "I guess I'm going to have to go find something for that fire."

Miss Sadie nodded. "Those men aren't going to be any help, that's for sure. Find whatever you can get your hands on for now. Brush, twigs. Let's just keep the little fire they do have built up enough to boil the onions; then we can worry about chopping fresh wood."

"All right," Ginger said. "I'll do my best."

In minutes, she returned with her arms filled with whatever she could find that might build up the fire.

In no time, Miss Sadie's onion broth scented the air, which was a mercy. For the past two hours, Ginger's senses had been violated with the nauseating smells of sickness and a camp in a general state of neglect, which she suspected would have been the case with or without cholera.

Miss Sadie planted her hands on her hips and looked around the camp in disgust. "While this soup boils, the two of us will need to gather up all the garbage these fellas have been collecting. Get a burn pile started, and at first light, we'll start chopping wood."

Ginger's stomach churned at the very thought of going near piles of animal bones, human waste and all manner of cans and skins. All the items this camp should have discarded long ago. But Ginger knew these men. They weren't ne'er-do-wells and thieves because they liked to work hard and take care of themselves. They didn't need to. When they ran out of provisions or something broke, they simply stole more. When they used up one area, they moved on, leaving it filthy and dilapidated. If Miss Sadie was right and cleanliness was, indeed, next to godliness, that explained a lot.

With a heavy sigh, she set about her task. Discarding everything from broken harnesses to filthy, oily horse blankets. She set aside a pile of broken wheels probably grabbed from broken-down wagons along the trail to start the blaze, as soon as she brought enough firewood to get it all burned.

Miss Sadie gave her a nod of approval as she dropped to the ground next to Yuley. "It's finished."

"Good. I've checked on all the men and taken stock of who's the sickest." She pointed toward Ames and Greely. "Nearest I can tell, those two are about as close to death as I've ever seen. Probably won't last through the night."

From his bedroll close to the fire, Yuley kept his gaze on her until Ginger's nerves reached the edge. "Yuley, what are you gawking at?"

The startled young man averted his gaze quickly. "Nothin', Miss Ginger. I reckon I was just lonesome for the sight of ya."

Ashamed of her snappiness, Ginger sent him an apologetic grin. "I missed you too, Yuley."

His sallow face brightened considerably. "No foolin'?"

"No foolin'."

The sound of a horse riding into camp interrupted the conversation. Yuley's demeanor changed from smiling to sober. Ginger turned, senses alerted. Her lip twitched with disdain as she watched Lane dismount and swagger toward her, carrying two enormous rabbits.

"So you didn't light out of here," she said. "I figured you were either dead or gone for good."

He scowled back at her. "And leave Web with all that . . ." He stopped abruptly as he noticed Miss Sadie. Her gray eyebrows were up, as she waited for him to finish his sentence. He sent her an insolent grin and tipped his hat. "Evenin', ma'am."

Miss Sadie *harrumph*ed and reached out for the rabbits.

"We'll take care of those. If you cook the way you clean up, they likely won't be edible."

Yuley snorted. Lane turned on him. "Shut up and take care of my horse, you dimwit."

"Don't talk to him that way," Ginger warned. "I mean it. And take care of your own horse. Yuley's sick."

But Yuley was already moving. "It's okay, Miss Ginger. He don't mean nothin' by it."

"Yeah, Miss Ginger. I don't mean nothing by it."

"Varmint."

Lane snatched her arm. "What was that, *Miss* Ginger?"

Slapping his hand away, Ginger glared. "You heard me. And keep your hands off me."

"What are you doing here, anyhow?" He wrinkled his nose, looking around, sniffing the air like a dog. "What is that stink?"

"You. Why don't you take a dadgum bath or stay upwind?"

He took a menacing step forward.

"Watch it, cowboy," Miss Sadie said with her own brand of menace. The quiet warning in her tone was enough to back a hungry bear away from a calf. Luckily, Lane was all coward at heart and backed down without a fight. Miss Sadie ladled out a bowl of onion soup and passed it to him. "Get this in your gullet."

"I ain't eatin' that. It stinks."

"Just eat it," Ginger said, exasperated. "We're trying to save your sorry hide." Miss Sadie passed the bowl over to her.

Ginger wrinkled her nose and shook her head. "Forget it."

"Take it." Miss Sadie's gaze took in a quick sweep of the camp. "Or do you want to end up like these men?"

"Can't I just wait and see if I start ailin'? I don't feel sick so far, except when I get close to Lane."

"You best stop insultin' me; I mean it." He looked back to Miss Sadie. "That's medicine for this?"

"Yes. Onion soup is a natural remedy that kills the cholera in most."

"Most?"

"Nothing is surefire but God."

He snorted. "I'd put a lot more stock in that nasty soup."

"Probably just as well, considering you're a lawless fool and all."

Surprisingly, he didn't comment as he took the bowl that Ginger still hadn't touched. "I'll eat it," he said. "But only 'cause I'm starvin' half to death, and it'll take awhile for you women to skin and cook them rabbits."

Ginger shoved her finger in his face. "We got better things to do than skin your rabbits. We got a camp full of sick men that need our attention. So you can just cook your own supper."

Miss Sadie placed a gentle hand on her arm. "Ginger, skin and roast the rabbits while I tend to these men. It ain't proper for you to be tendin' them that close anyhow."

Ginger drew back, a frown pushing her eyebrows together. "Why not?"

"Because you're a young and unmarried. Like I said—not proper. Not if you want to make a decent marriage."

Lane tossed back his head and howled. "Our Ginger . . . proper?"

"Shut up, Lane," Ginger growled. Then she turned back to Miss Sadie. "That's dumb. I've been tending these men and their wounds and sicknesses since I was small."

"Well, that may be. But you're not going to do anything improper while I'm in charge of you."

Ginger planted her hands on her hips. "What do you mean, in charge?"

Miss Sadie dipped another ladle of the broth into a bowl they'd brought with them and shoved it toward Ginger. "You know exactly what I mean. I'm here to keep an eye on you and to make sure you don't get yourself hurt or compromised. Take this."

Stunned to silence, Ginger could do nothing but accept the foul-smelling soup and plop herself down on the ground by the fire.

Miss Sadie nodded. "Good girl. Finish all that broth and then get to work on the rabbits." She turned to Lane. "We'd be obliged if you'd get some wood for the fire."

A short laugh left his throat. "I bet you would. But I don't do firewood. I've been out huntin' all day, and I need my rest. And I'm gonna sit right here and stretch out my legs until those rabbits are roasted real nice and hot."

"I'll get it, ma'am," Dale said. He tossed Lane a look of disgust.

Ginger's heart softened. "I appreciate the offer, Dale, but you're too sick."

"We have plenty cut not far from here, Ginger. If you think you could walk with me, we can carry it back."

"Just tell me where it is, and I'll go."

Lane jumped up. "Sit down old man," he sneered at Dale. "I'll help her."

Ginger scowled and almost told him just what he could do with his offer of help, but she knew they could get twice as much wood over in camp if they worked together. As distasteful as that thought was to her, she knew it was best.

Dale's chest was puffed, and he tensed for a fight he could never win in this condition. She placed a hand on his shoulder. "It's okay, Dale. We'll go get it. Are you strong enough to skin the rabbits while I'm getting wood?"

He nodded. "I can do that." Glancing up to Lane, he added, "I won't be sick forever. You best watch yourself, boy."

"Let's go," Ginger broke in before Lane took advantage of the weakened old man and things got out of hand.

"You know," Lane said leaning close to her. "You don't have to worry none about all that proper talk."

"What are you talking about, Lane?" Ginger walked around a tree stump, noting the woodpile she would have seen if the sun wasn't gone.

"Well, you know you're gettin' married no matter what."

A short laugh burst from her. "Oh, yeah? What are you a fortune-teller now?"

He stopped in his tracks and grabbed her arms, bringing her close to him. His breath so close to her face nearly gagged her. "You know dern well your pa promised you to me long ago. Soon as you get back for good and this wagon train job is over, we're finding a preacher."

"You're dumb as a boulder." Ginger ignored the warning in his eyes. "I ain't marrying the likes of you. I'd die first."

"Oh, yes you are. And you better watch how you talk to me. I been waitin' a long time for you. And I'm gettin' mighty restless. I might just forget my manners one of these days."

"Are you threatening me?"

"Call it whatever you want. But don't insult me again." He kissed her hard. Ginger struggled against him until he finally released her. She rubbed her hand across her mouth hard, trying to remove the feel and smell. "Do that again," she said coldly, "and you'll wish cholera had gotten to you."

"Ginger!" Miss Sadie's voice called from camp. "Where's that wood?"

"Coming, Miss Sadie."

She gathered an armload of wood while Lane stood watching her. It took all of her strength to walk past him on her way back to the campfire. "You're mine, gal. You best get it through your head."

Ginger didn't respond, but her knees felt weak. How could Web have promise her to Lane? Lane must be holding something over his head. It was the only thing that made sense. If they made it out of this alive, she had every intention of finding out exactly what he was thinking.

One thing was certain: she would not be marrying Lane Conners. She meant what she'd said. She'd die first.

Ten

Grant barely had a chance to worry about Ginger in the hours after she and Miss Sadie left. Jenny Shewmate's baby was stillborn two hours before Jenny herself succumbed to cholera. He hadn't even had time to help with the burying. Now, hours later, he stumbled out of Blake's tent after tending Fannie's little brother Kip who so far had only a mild case, so Grant had used the onion soup.

He walked slowly—stumbled was more like it—toward his tent, hoping for a couple of hours of sleep before beginning the next round of treatment, when Amanda Kane stopped him. He tensed, still leery of this woman who had only recently come out of a bad addiction to laudanum. "Everything okay, Mrs. Kane?"

"Yes."

"Then what can I do for you?"

Surely she wasn't going to beg for the drug. He knew they'd all been under enormous pressure, but he wouldn't give in to her.

"You're exhausted, and I want to help you."

Taken aback, Grant allowed a second of shame for his suspicion. "Are you sure?" It made sense. Amanda was without family. Unless you counted Charles Harrison, who was besotted with the widow and wanted to marry her.

"It's the least I can do." She'd caused a lot of trouble in her quest for more laudanum a while back, but Grant couldn't let her do this as penance.

"Amanda, your plan to trade Toni didn't work. Everything is fine, and you're forgiven. There's no need to risk your life to try to make up for all that."

Only Amanda's addiction to laudanum had compelled her to betray Toni and lead kidnappers to her. But thankfully, the plan had failed, Amanda had broken her habit and had been forgiven by everyone involved. Now, she had to forgive herself.

In the moonlight, the quick tears in her eyes sparkled like jewels. "You know I have no family. I want to help. Please, accept my help and don't judge my reasons."

After only a second more of hesitation, he nodded. "I was going to sleep for awhile, but we could start the regimen over. Whatever you do, don't let Buddy help if he tries. I sent him to bed two hours ago. I want him to get a full night's sleep, or he might relapse."

She nodded. "I understand."

"Go to Yellow Bird's tent. She has the broth boiling. Feed each sick person as much as they'll take. If the patient's limbs turn dark, come get me, we'll need to use quinine."

"Thank you for trusting me," she said, her lip quivering with self-condemnation.

"I need your help," he said, aware of the lack of emotion in his voice. He was simply too exhausted. "Come and get me if you need me. Otherwise, let me sleep for three hours."

With a nod, she set off toward Yellow Bird's campfire.

A soft snow began to fall as Grant continued his way to his tent. He cast a glance at the starless sky. They were never going to make it over the mountains. He knew it; Blake knew it; and the wagon train folks were beginning to grumble about it. There had been too many delays. Too much tragedy. It seemed like the westward trek was cursed.

A hulking shadow fell across his path, pulling him from his thoughts. "You look deep in thought, Doc. I said hello three times, and you didn't say a word back." Grant tensed as Web fell into step beside him.

"Sorry," he muttered. "I'm just on my way to get some sleep. Do you need anything?"

"Sure do. I noticed that pretty Mrs. Kane and you was awfully deep in conversation just a few minutes ago." Web gave him a nudge. "You, uh, got plans for that one?"

Every nerve in Grant's body pulled back in revulsion. Sheer willpower alone kept Grant from walking off. "No. And if I did, I wouldn't discuss it with another man. That wouldn't be gentlemanly."

"Oh, sure, sure." Web nodded. "I reckon I know exactly what you mean. A fella just can't help but wonder about a pretty widow meetin' up with a man, such as yourself, after dark and all."

The man was fishing, but Grant was too tired to be evasive and risk camp gossip. "She wants to help with the sick members of the wagon train. That's all."

Web's eyes took on a smug sheen. "That's what I figured. The woman has a heart of gold."

"Yeah, she's a regular saint." Grant gave a weary sigh. "If that's all, I'll say goodnight."

"Well, now." Web rubbed the stubble on his chin. "I was thinking, maybe I'll go help Mrs. Kane. She could probably use a hand if you're gonna sleep and all."

Grant's anger rose hot and quick. "If you want to help anyone, why don't you hightail it back to that camp of yours and help your daughter?"

Web dropped the dumb suitor act and pushed his bushy eyebrows together. "What are you sayin'? My girl's back at the camp? What's she doin' over there?"

"She and Miss Sadie took the wagon and drove to your camp where at least some of the men have cholera. But I guess you already know they're sick, since your son brought the illness to our camp."

In a flash, Web reached out and grabbed the front of his shirt. "You blamin' this on my boy?"

Grant knew he had said too much. He could kick himself for being so reckless. He shook his head. "I'm just a tired doctor that has seen too much death today. But I think a decent father would want to go and get his daughter out of harm's way."

"Harm? My men know better than to lay a finger on her."

"Are you sure about that?"

Doubt flickered in the man's eyes. Grant's stomach turned over with dread. "Don't you think you ought to ride over there and make sure she's all right?"

Web peered closer. "What's your interest in that girl? You sweet on her?"

The question caught Grant by surprise. "My interest?"

"Yeah. You sweet on her or somethin'?" Anger burned in the man's eyes.

"I just think a man ought to look after his daughter. So I'll say again, instead of tagging along after Amanda Kane—who, incidentally, is being courted by Mr. Harrison—why don't you ride to your camp and help your own daughter like any decent father would?"

All the pretense was gone from Web now. His lips curled. "If you knew what she really came here to do, you wouldn't be wanting me to save her."

Grant's mind barely worked after thirty-six hours without sleep, but he couldn't let the comment go unchallenged. "Are you going to tell me what you mean?"

"No. I don't guess I better. Not just yet, anyhow." He spat a stream of tobacco juice to the ground, narrowly missing Grant's boot. "If you'll pardon me, Doc, I'm gonna go see if a pretty widow could use a hand."

He was slightly hunched over and Grant noted the way he had a tendency to press a hand to his side as he sauntered off, leaving Grant to mull over the implication. Web wasn't well. That had been obvious from the beginning, but it wasn't cholera.

Grant had other things to worry about right now when it came to that man. Obviously, Grant had given away the fact that he knew Web was in the wagon train under false pretenses. That was bad enough, but Web seemed to be implying that Ginger was involved in whatever plot the outlaw band was planning.

Blake was going to have to do something about Web soon, before the man brought even more disaster on the wagon train. Grant debated whether or not to go straight to Blake but decided against it. The wagon master had been busy since sunup, consoling the grieving families of the dead, as well as Fannie—they were both worried sick about Kip. It would have to wait until morning.

Moments later, he entered his tent and fell onto his bedroll without even removing his boots. The last thing he heard before he drifted to sleep was Web's accusatory words against Ginger.

What on earth was that girl up to? All he knew for now was that he missed her more than he'd ever thought possible and maybe Web was right. Maybe he was sweet on Ginger Freeman. Even after the dark, anguished day he'd just endured, the crazy thought made him smile just before sleep claimed his weary mind.

Ginger woke to Yuley singing "Rock of Ages." She sat up and stared at Miss Sadie, who stood over the coffeepot. The older woman shook her head and looked to where Dale slept. "Poor man didn't make it."

Trying to wrap her head around the meaning of Miss Sadie's words, Ginger's eyes followed where her finger pointed. Dale lay unmoving on his bedroll, his eyes closed, face serene.

As her mind cleared of sleep, Ginger realized Yuley was singing "Rock of Ages," a favorite hymn of the Sunday gatherings on the wagon train. She wasn't sure why he would choose that one instead of "Amazing Grace" like they'd sung at all the burials since she joined the pioneers. More than likely it was the only hymn he knew.

His eyes were watery when he looked at her. He stopped singing. "I reckon he done died, Miss Ginger."

"I reckon he did," she said softly. "I'm sorry, Yuley. I know Dale was good to you." She turned to Miss Sadie. "What about the rest of the men and Elijah?"

"Elijah's hanging on. And no one else has died."

"Dale didn't seem that sick, Miss Sadie. Less than the others. Even Yuley."

A shrug lifted Miss Sadie's shoulders as she handed Ginger a cup of steaming brew. "Cholera can happen that fast." Something about the way she looked extra hard at her made Ginger wonder just what the older woman had going on in her head.

Ginger's icy fingers wrapped around the warm cup, and she brought the steam close to her face to warm her nose. "It must have dropped another twenty degrees." Snow blanketed the ground. "I'm stretching the canvas back on the wagon, and that's where we'll sleep tonight, Miss Sadie."

"Left it back at camp."

"Oh, that's right."

"Besides, we'll have to bury him and get the burn pile going today. There's no time to sashay back to camp."

Ginger glanced around. "Where's Lane?"

Miss Sadie's lip curled in disdain. "He lit out sometime during the night. Took most of the onions."

Indignation fired through her chest. "What are you saying? He just left us and took the medicine?"

"That's it."

"Then I'll have to go back to camp, Miss Sadie. We need more onions, or there's no point in being here."

"Simmer down." Miss Sadie stirred the pot on the fire then straightened up, pressing her hands into the small of her back. "I said he took most of them. But not all. I kept some stashed in the wagon, and he didn't get those. If the broth is going to work at all, we have enough. If it isn't, one more isn't going to make a difference."

Ginger sipped her coffee in silence, trying to avoid looking at Dale. Finally, she couldn't sit there any longer, knowing a dead man lay only a few feet from her. She set down her cup. "Yuley, where's the shovel?"

He'd been singing quietly and he stopped mid-song to give her a blank stare.

"A shovel, Yuley." Making shoveling motions with both hands, she kept her gaze fixed on his. "You know what a shovel is, right?"

His face brightened. "Yep. You dig with it."

"That's right." Thank goodness. One just never knew how much actually got through that head of his. "Where is it?"

Frowning, he looked at the ground, clearly concentrating. "Oh, that's right."

"What's right?"

"Dale broke it over Clay Jones's back one day."

Miss Sadie let out an exasperated breath. "Land sakes."

"Yes ma'am."

Incredulous, Ginger shook her head. "Do you mean to tell me you have nothing to bury this man with?"

Yuley took another breath, scratched his greasy head and then stared at her helplessly. "I reckon there ain't nothing."

Yuley inched closer to Dale's body. "I can try to dig with my hands."

Miss Sadie stooped down and took Yuley by the shoulders. "You'll do no such thing. Now come over by the fire and get warm. It's time for your medicine."

Yuley wrinkled his nose. "Yes ma'am." The hesitation in his voice made Ginger grin.

"It's not much good, is it?"

He cast a quick glance at Miss Sadie. "Well, it ain't so bad."

A chuckle left the older woman as she gaze at him with maternal fondness, handing him a bowl of the foul soup. "It's okay, Yuley. This isn't meant to taste good. You get yourself better, and I'll make you a real meal."

"I'd be obliged, ma'am."

Miss Sadie turned back to Ginger, jerking her head to motion her away from the fire. Ginger followed, and they headed to the wagon before speaking. "Looks like you'll have to go back to the camp, after all."

"It appears that way."

"We'll need a couple of tents. I don't want these men sleeping in the snow."

"There aren't any?" It had been too dark the night before to bother looking.

"Now, do you think if these men had tents, they'd be sleeping on the ground on a cold night like last night?"

"I did," Ginger shot back.

"Well, let's not argue about it."

"We'll need two tents. One for you and me and one for those men. And a shovel. And you should bring more blankets if anyone can spare any. The ones these men are using are going to need to be burned. They're beyond washing, and even if they weren't, they're so threadbare, they wouldn't hold up to a good scrubbing, anyway."

After a bowl of the nasty broth and a biscuit, Ginger climbed into the wagon seat and began the two-hour ride to the wagon train.

She arrived before noon and went straight to Blake's camp. Fannie sat on a barrel, her small hands wrapped around a cup of coffee. She barely acknowledged Ginger as she stared ahead, her face ashen.

Toni stood over the fire, tending a pot of the familiar-smelling soup. "How is everything at the camp?"

Ginger gave her a quick rundown, leaving Lane Conners out of it. "But I'm going to need a few things—a shovel to bury the man that died in the night, some blankets, and two tents. We can use Miss Sadie's for one. Is Yellow Bird tucked in with you?"

"Yes, the tent is empty. But it's still up. You'll need to take it down and roll it up."

Ginger cast a glance at Fannie. "Do you think Kip and Buddy could manage to get it pulled down and loaded into the wagon for me?"

Tears sprang to Fannie's eyes, and she buried her face in her hands. Toni went to her and wrapped her small frame in her arms.

"What's going on?" Ginger planted her hands on her hips. "I mean it. Tell me."

Toni frowned up at her. "Ginger," she said keeping her voice soft, her tone even. "Kip is ill with cholera. He took sick yesterday, and he's getting worse instead of better."

The news struck Ginger in her core, robbing her of breath. Which was probably just as well, while Fannie sobbed her frustration and worry into Toni's shoulder. When the tears were spent, Ginger had regained her speech. "Well, once you start giving him that soup of Miss Sadie's, he'll perk right up. You'll see."

Fannie jerked her head up and flashed angry eyes. "Oh, Ginger, stop trying to sound cheerful. Maybe God wants to take Kip like he took my mama and pa. Maybe He'll want to take Katie, too, and then Blake and my baby. How would you know? How would you know anything about anything?"

The anger in her tone paralyzed Ginger. She couldn't move or speak. Wasn't sure what to do. Toni gave her a sympathetic smile but didn't bother to take up for her. But Ginger understood—or thought she did. "I guess I best be going." She paused, then went to Fannie and touched her shoulder. "Don't worry. I won't hold it against you, you hollering at me like that. I had all that anger inside me, too, when it was Buddy laying there sick, and there was nothing I could do to make him well."

Fannie reached up and grabbed onto Ginger's hand.

Grabbed it so hard in fact, Ginger realized she'd underesti-
mated her friend's strength. "Thank you, Ginger."

"Ginger, I have a shovel in my things," Toni said. "You're
welcome to borrow it. And there are a couple of extra blankets in there, too."

"I'm obliged. Do you know of an extra tent around camp?"

Toni averted her gaze. "I don't know if it's proper or not."

"What?"

"The entire Shewmate family is gone."

"Jenny?" Ginger sucked in a breath. "But she was going to
have a baby."

Toni's gaze was sober, sad. "I know. Barnabas took sick
before we even buried Jenny. Grant said he must have been
hiding it for as long as he could. By the time he got really
sick, it was too late."

Then what good was the quinine or onion soup if folks
were just going to die anyway? Before Ginger could voice her
sentiment, Fannie gathered a weary breath. "I'll talk to Blake
about giving you the tent. He and some of the other men are
burying Barnabas right now."

With the news of such a senseless tragedy, Ginger lost
any desire she'd had for conversation. "I'll be back after I've
loaded up all the other things Miss Sadie's needing."

She walked back through camp without stopping to
speak with anyone. Not that she'd been invited to any fires
anyway. It seemed that almost every family in the wagon
train was boiling onions. Were they all affected? She reached
the empty camp Yellow Bird and Miss Sadie had shared. An
eerie silence permeated the air, and the unmistakable stench

of cholera. Suddenly Ginger's stomach revolted, and she dropped to her knees as the retching began.

She barely felt a hand on her head, but somehow she was aware that someone knelt beside her. When she was spent, she lay on her side. Shivering in the snow, miserable, aching.

Strong arms lifted her, and she was being carried, snuggled against a warm chest, which rumbled as he prayed, "Lord, not this. Please don't take another woman from me."

Eleven

"Nothing more than a weak stomach and exhaustion." Grant smiled to himself as he announced the diagnosis to Ginger the next morning after she'd gotten a full night of sleep. Slept like the dead, as a matter of fact, on a thick pallet in Miss Sadie's tent. He would have taken her to his own tent, but the outcry of propriety would have forced him to bring her back anyway. He'd posted Buddy at her side and had checked on her himself every hour.

She gave him a sheepish grin. "I feel plumb stupid, Grant."

"Well, don't. Feel blessed. A lot of people in this wagon train would gladly trade cholera for a little embarrassment."

Her face reddened. "I didn't mean that." She flipped her long braid from her shoulder so that it rested in the gentle curve at the small of her back. "How's Kip?"

"Showing improvement, praise the Lord."

She nodded solemnly without her usual snort. "Is Sam having a service today, this being the Lord's Day and all?"

"Yes. We almost cancelled, but Sam felt the folks might need a service more than ever."

"I'd like to attend myself, but I don't suppose I should leave Miss Sadie any longer. It snowed again last night."

"Don't worry. Toni told us what you were needing. Mr. Harrison volunteered to haul all the supplies. Your pa went with him to show him the way. All you'll need to take back is your tent, here."

Ginger gasped and turned on him fiercely, groaning. "Oh, Grant. Don't you have a brain in your head?"

Stung, Grant frowned. "It might interest you to know that I see it as a good sign that Web volunteered to go with him. He seems to have taken a genuine liking to Mr. Harrison. Maybe a real friend will help him want to be a better man."

A bitter laugh flew from her as she slipped past him, ducking through the flap carrying all the blankets, which were the only items still left inside the tent.

Grant followed. "What are you laughing at?"

"You don't know very many outlaws, do you?"

"A lot more lately than I ever planned to know on a first-name basis."

She had the good grace to blush but set about taking down the tent. Grant helped, yanking up stakes and finally helping her roll the tent and load it into the wagon. He slipped the yoke around the oxen's neck.

"Don't bother just yet."

"I thought you were all fired up to go back?"

"I might as well take the time to ask for help from the Almighty. I'm going to need all the help I can get."

"Don't worry, Ginger. This'll all be over soon. I didn't have any new cases this morning."

"That's a mercy."

"Toni says you should come have breakfast with her and Yellow Bird." Grant still wondered what had upset Ginger so about Mr. Harrison and Web taking supplies to Miss Sadie. In his mind's eye, he recalled Web's warning that Ginger had an ulterior motive for being part of the wagon train. Most likely, Web was just trying to divert suspicion from his own slimy carcass to his daughter. As much as he hated to bury his head in the sand, he couldn't believe Ginger would be so deceptive. She was too open—spoke every thought in her head, more often than not. And sometimes too much so. In light of that, Grant had a hard time believing she was hiding anything.

"You coming?"

Ginger's question caught him off guard and pulled him away from his thoughts. He shook his head. "I have some rounds to make before the service. I'll see you a little later."

He hesitated as she walked away. Then a burst of energy lifted his spirit and caught his voice. "Ginger!" he called.

Her eyebrows lifted. "Forget something?"

"Not really." He swallowed hard. Was he really ready to do this? Maybe there were too many questions in his head for him to hear his heart clearly.

"Grant?" Her voice was just soft enough to show him the gentle, womanly Ginger that he'd caught a glimpse of on occasion. The woman he had trouble banishing from his mind.

"I'd like to sit with you at the gathering, if you don't mind."

"Why would I?" She gave him a frown that clearly said she thought he might be daft.

Grant's ears heated up despite the snow flurries flying about the air. "Well, I mean . . ." What exactly did he mean? Suddenly he wasn't sure.

"Last I heard, this is a free country. Sit wherever you want." At this return of the gruffer Ginger, he was almost glad she'd misunderstood his intent.

"Okay. I will," he said. He cleared his throat. "Thanks."

"Is there anything else, Grant? I'm pretty hungry. Besides, I don't want to keep Toni waiting."

"That's it." Deflated, Grant turned and headed back to Miss Sadie's wagon where he'd left his bag while he helped Ginger with the tent. That definitely hadn't gone as he'd hoped. Probably just as well. A cholera epidemic probably wasn't the most appropriate time to start courting a girl. But mercy, did she have to act like she didn't know that he was asking for more than a seat next to her at a church meeting?

"What's so funny?" Ginger demanded around a bite of cornbread from last night's dinner. Toni was giggling outright, and Yellow Bird smiled quietly as she sat cross legged in the tent nursing Little Sam.

Toni handed her a cup of coffee. "Grant asked you to sit with him at the meeting?"

"Well, I don't see what's so funny about that."

"Are you truly that backward, my friend?"

Incensed, Ginger set her cup on the ground. "I don't think I care to sit here and be insulted." She shoved up from the ground.

"Oh, sit back down, you silly girl." Toni filled her own cup and sat close to the fire. "Don't you know why Grant asked you?"

"I couldn't figure at first," Ginger said. She lowered herself to the ground once again and retrieved her cup. "But the more I thought on it, the more I realized he most likely didn't want to have to stand through the whole service. He's doing rounds, you know. I reckon he might be late."

Toni shook her head. "Ginger, when a man asks a woman if he can accompany her to a church meeting, it means he'd like to court her."

A thick chunk of cornbread made a detour down her throat and lodged in a bad place, choking Ginger. She started to cough, robbed of air as her mind raged against the information

"Grant!" she sputtered. "You're crazy. That's not what he meant."

"Want me to ask him?" Toni's smug look held no doubt whatsoever.

"No!"

"Admit it, then. You know that's what Grant meant. He wants to court you."

Yellow Bird switched the baby to the other side. "The doctor is a good man."

Ginger gulped down another swig of coffee. "That's your opinion," she muttered. But she knew it wasn't fair to leave the comment hanging in the air like that. Especially when he'd helped save Buddy's life and had worked himself exhausted to doctor the wagon train. "Well, he is a good man, but that's not the point."

Toni set the pot back on the fire and faced ginger. "I don't know why you continue to pretend there's nothing between you and Grant. Anyone with eyes can see how he looks at you."

Ginger's stomach jumped, and she took another gulp. It just couldn't be. How could she have been foolish enough to let Grant think he had a right to want to court her? It was one thing for her to give up her desire for revenge. But the thought of Grant as more than . . . well, it's not that she'd never thought of it. And it wasn't as repulsive to consider as Lane, for instance, but still . . .

She set her empty cup on the ground and jumped up.

Maybe she had somehow given Grant the wrong idea about the nature of their relationship, but she could certainly do something to discourage him from taking it any farther.

Without a word to Toni or Yellow Bird, she ducked out of the tent into the frigid October air and started walking. She wasn't sure where she was headed, but one thing was for sure, she wouldn't return until she'd found Grant and told him a thing or two!

An explosion of pain hit Web as he bent over to pour coffee into Miss Sadie's cup. He couldn't hold back a groan as the liquid nearly spilled out onto her lap.

"Land sakes, Web Freeman. Give me that before you burn the hide off your hand." Miss Sadie took the pot from him and stood up. "Sit down."

Dadburn, that woman was one for giving orders. He'd never taken orders from anyone, let alone a female, but just now, sitting seemed like the best thing for him to do. She sashayed to the fire and set the coffee pot next to the pot of soup. When she returned, she stood over him, hands on her wide hips and gave him that no-nonsense look he usually hated on a woman's face. "I know you don't have cholera. It don't act this way. What ails you, Web?"

Wincing, he reached out and grabbed her wrist. "Don't talk so loud. Do you want to tell the whole camp I'm sick?"

She dropped to the bench that Yuley had fashioned for her out of some old, abandoned wagon parts. "All right." She kept her voice low as though she understood his position. "Now, tell me what you have."

He'd kept his pain to himself for so long, now that it was impossible to hide, he felt naked. "I don't rightly know what it is. I been hurtin' worse and worse for a while now. And it's where I can't do . . ." Well, if she were the type of woman he usually associated with, he wouldn't much care whether he offended her or not. But something about her way made him want to mind his manners.

"Can't do what?"

He blew out a breath as the pain began to subside. "Go."

She peered closer. "You want me to go away?"

Rolling his eyes, he leaned in closer. "I can't go . . . to the outhouse. If you catch my meanin'." And he sure hoped she would.

Her eyes grew wide, but that was the only indication that she might be a little shocked by his admission. Decent folks just didn't talk about such things. Even he knew that. But she shouldn't have asked if she didn't want to know. "Did you talk to Doctor Kelley?"

The thought of the man left a bitter taste in Web's mouth. "No, ma'am, and I don't intend to." Not after the way he implied Web wasn't being a proper pa by letting Ginger go off alone to nurse the men. When had that girl ever listened to him in the first place? As a matter of fact, after she helped him with this last job, he was going to cut her loose to go west or do whatever she wanted to do.

Miss Sadie scrutinized him, then sipped her coffee. She shrugged. "I reckon that's your call."

"Hold on a minute. What do you think ails me?"

She shrugged. "I'm not a doctor. But I've seen similar symptoms before. The good parson back home got a wasting sickness. Held onto his side just like you do. Sometimes he'd get to hurting so bad, he'd faint dead away."

Luckily for Web, that had only happened once, and no one had paid him any mind. Thought he'd taken a nap.

"A wasting sickness, ya say?"

Web's heart sank. If he had what Miss Sadie suggested, there wasn't much point in stealing Harrison's money. He wouldn't be around to spend it, anyway.

Twelve

Kip Caldwell was finally out of the woods. The combination of onion soup and doses of quinine had killed the cholera that threatened to eat away at his insides. In the last few hours, he'd managed to keep a few bites of the soup down and several swallows of water. Not a lot, but infinitely better than before when he became violently ill from the smallest sip of water into his mouth.

Buddy looked down at his pale, sleeping friend and shook his head. "I sure hope he pulls through like I did." His voice cracked, and Grant suspected it had little to do with adolescent changing and more to do with the weight of responsibility bearing down on the poor lad. Grant's heart went out to him. "This isn't your fault, Buddy."

Tears shot to his eyes. "I was sick when I got to camp. If it wasn't for me, no one else would have taken sick and died." Angrily, he swiped away the tears that were making rapid trails down his cheeks.

"You didn't do it on purpose." Grant slipped the bottle of quinine back into his bag. "No one blames you."

But he knew that wasn't true. Plenty of folks, mainly those who had lost loved ones, did blame Buddy. Grant had even heard Ginger's name grumbled about, since she and Buddy were kin. Blake had put out a half a dozen fires from people who wanted to send the Freemans packing. Only the fact that Ginger had been such a help to so many people and had brought in so much meat kept the grumbling from escalating into something more.

Buddy jammed his hands into his trouser pockets and shook his head with determination. "I'm going to make it up to him. To all of the folks who've lost family."

"You're doing a fine job already, Buddy. I don't know what I'd have done without your help over the last couple of days. And you were barely off your own sickbed and still weak as a newborn colt. So you just consider your debt to this wagon train paid in full and be proud of yourself."

Even though his eyes remained moist and his voice quivered, he seemed to perk up at Grant's words as they headed toward the tent flap.

"You think I could be a doctor?"

Grant slipped outside and held the flap for the boy. "I don't see why not. You'll need some schooling. But you're a bright young man; I'm sure you'd do well."

Buddy's face clouded. "I don't see how I could ever go to college. I doubt Pa would let me."

Grant clapped his hand on Buddy's shoulder. "Don't fret about it for now. You have plenty of time. How about if I loan you a couple of my medical books?"

And just like that, the cloud lifted from Buddy's expression, and his eyes lit up. "Yes, sir! I'd like that a lot."

"All right then. Go and get cleaned up and ready for the service, and I'll pick out a book and bring it with me to the meeting."

"Yes sir!" Buddy took off at a run. Grant smiled to himself. The boy's skin practically hung on his bones from his illness, but then, he hadn't been that nourished before cholera, if Grant had to guess. He made a mental note to see to it that Buddy received extra food. With Web and Miss Sadie gone, and Ginger leaving again right after the service today, he figured he'd have to appeal to some of the women of the train, such as Mrs. Kane and Toni, to make sure the boy was fed regular and nourishing meals.

"Grant Kelley!" The sound of Ginger's angry voice stopped Grant in his tracks and all thoughts of Buddy's wellbeing fled from his mind. He whipped around, conscious of the way his heartbeat picked up at the sight of her shapely figure filling out a buckskin shirt and trousers. It had been said around camp that Ginger wasn't womanly—folks had gone so far as to say she wanted to look like a man—but never was Grant more aware of her femininity than now as she approached him, her eyes flashing, her braid bouncing with each step.

"Something wrong?" He tensed. When she was angry, and the anger seemed pointed in his direction, it was never good to let down his guard.

"Yes." Her shoulders squared, and she narrowed her gaze. "Toni says . . ."

Her hesitation intrigued him. Ginger was rarely at a loss for words. Not that her words always made sense, but she wasn't the type to weigh her thoughts before she expressed them.

"Toni says what?" So help him, he couldn't help finding her adorable even now when her nose was in the air and her lips were pinched like a Boston schoolmarm. And he'd seen his share of those growing up in the East.

His grin seemed to be just the nudge she needed. "Toni says when you asked me if you could sit with me at the service . . ." She paused again—this time, her face flushed, and she averted her gaze.

He felt his own neck heat up at her words. It wasn't exactly proper for her to bring it up. Besides, he was still feeling a little stung by her nonchalant response to his request.

"What are you trying to say, Ginger?"

She gathered an enormous breath, and he could see by the rise in her chest that she was about to just let him have it. He braced himself as she let the breath go amid an onslaught of words. "Toni said you were asking me if you could come courting. Is that true?" Without awaiting a response, she continued, stepping even closer to him, which made it a little difficult for him to concentrate on what she was spouting. Clearly unaware of this fact, she continued. "Because if it is—and you'd best not call Toni a liar or you'll answer to me—if it is, you can just forget it, because I'm not interested in being courted by you or anyone else. But especially you." Her expression softened a little, and she hesitated for the merest of seconds. "Well, not *especially* you. Just anyone."

Even through the knowledge that she didn't want anything to do with him, Grant felt a surge of affection for this little hothead. Especially after she backtracked, as though afraid of hurting his feelings.

How could a woman not understand the rituals associated with courting? He understood that she'd been raised in a camp full of outlaw men, but he'd always just figured women were born knowing how to manipulate romantic situations. Something about this situation just delighted him. That delight, combined with the surge of affection, was the only thing he could attribute his next actions to. Bending forward, he took her hands in his and pressed a kiss to the startled girl's cheek before she could duck away.

She yanked her hands away, and one palm flew to her cheek as she stepped back, staring at him with wild, enormous eyes. "I—how—" Even her sputtering seemed adorable to him.

"How dare you kiss me!"

Outraged, she seemed to be struggling for breath. His fingers gently encircled her upper arm. "Ginger, relax."

Predictably, she jerked away. "Don't tell me to relax, you . . . you . . ."

"Cad?"

"Worse than that! But I won't say it in front of these good, Christian folks."

Grant glanced about and sure enough, they were beginning to draw a crowd of curious onlookers. Some looked amused, some indignant. Some indifferent. But Grant wasn't about to look like a fool in front of a crowd. He raised his hand. "It's all right, folks," he said. "We're just going to check on Kip Caldwell."

He took her by the arm and led her to the tent, away from prying eyes. Surprisingly enough, she didn't protest as he pulled back the tent flap and hung back for her to duck in ahead of him.

"Now, look," he said, before she could light into him again. "I'm sorry for giving you a peck on the cheek, okay? It was only because I found it endearing that you didn't know I was trying to court you."

Her blush deepened. "So you were mocking me?"

"Of course not. Why do you always get offended over the wrong things?"

"I don't." She folded her arms across her chest. "I only get offended when men kiss me without my permission. Don't I have a right to say who gets that close to me?"

Her chin began to quiver. Grant fought hard against pulling her to him. "Again, I apologize. It wasn't very honorable of me not to ask permission first."

She narrowed her gaze. "Really?"

Grant supposed since surrender wasn't really within her realm of behavior, she had a hard time accepting an apology. "Really. Now, let's discuss the reason you came to see me in the first place.

Her expression grew blank. "What reason?" Then her eyes lit. "Oh, yeah. You want to court me. Is that true?"

"What if it were true?" Grant's heart slammed against his chest. But he'd already set something into motion, and whatever the outcome, he couldn't back out now. Actually, she'd already said she didn't want anyone courting her. Now he felt foolish.

Ginger seemed just as nervous, as she gathered in a gulp of air and her eyes widened.

"Is it true?" Her tone had dropped, and she didn't seem nearly as defensive.

Grant took heart. Rather than risk spooking her, Grant kept his distances and didn't give into the temptation to take her hands again. "I guess it is."

Her expression fell. Her soft, brown eyes sought his understanding. "You shouldn't even think about me that way, Grant. It's not possible."

"It could be, couldn't it?" The fact that she hadn't started yelling bolstered his courage. "Unless Web was right, and you're promised to someone else."

Shock froze her expression for a split second. "What's Web got to do with this? You been talking to him about me?"

"Not really. I just thought he should have gone with you to make sure you were safe, and he told me to keep my nose out of his business. He seemed to think my interest in you was a little more than casual, so he took it upon himself to tell me you were promised to a man in his gang."

"Well, I'm not. Lane Conners makes me sick, and I don't know why Web promised him I'd marry him some day, because I'd die first."

Her impassioned words left no doubt in Grant's mind that she meant exactly what she said. The thought both lifted his spirits and worried him. What if Web pressed the matter with her? Would she feel compelled to give in? Despite the distance she kept from Web, he still seemed to have a hold over her.

"Maybe you shouldn't be the one to take the tent back

to Miss Sadie. What if you stay and let one of the other women—Amanda Kane maybe—take your place?"

She waved away his concern. "Don't worry. Lane high-tailed it out of camp night before last. I doubt he'll be back."

He'd been thinking more of Web, but the way her thoughts went straight to Lane worried him. Plus, even though she'd said the words with seeming conviction, a hint of doubt flashed in her eyes, and Grant wasn't convinced. "Maybe you shouldn't go anyway."

"I'm going." Her determination reminded him of the way Fannie had stood up to Blake two nights before so she could be with Jenny Shewmate while she gave birth. Ginger had the same indomitable spirit as the wagon master's bride. The kind of spirit a woman needed to survive out west. Someone who wouldn't run away or shrink back when hardship came. Someone who could smile at a baby and stand loyally beside a friend. Or a husband. The kind of woman he needed for his wife.

"Why are you staring at me?" Ginger's voice yanked him from his thoughts.

Before he could answer, light streamed into the tent as the flap opened and Fannie slipped inside as though his thoughts had summoned her. She looked from Grant to Ginger. "Am I interrupting?"

Ginger shook her head

Fannie turned to Grant. "How's Kip?"

Barely able to concentrate on the patient or Fannie's question, Grant forced himself to focus. "He's getting better. But he'll need to stay in bed and take the broth. He'll be weak for a while. But I believe he'll pull through."

Fannie's weary body slumped with relief. "Praise God."

Ginger smiled and slipped her arm around Fannie's shoulders. "You see, I told you Grant would get him through this."

Her words rammed Grant, square in the gut.

Fannie grinned. "You sure did. Even when I wasn't being very nice to you."

A blush stained Ginger's cheeks. "I told you I wasn't going to hold it against you, didn't I?"

Grant took in this exchange between the two women. The fact that Ginger hadn't, at the very least, given Fannie a good piece of her mind indicated what he'd believed for a long time. Ginger Freeman had more potential than anyone gave her credit for. Once a person chipped away to the heart of the matter, she would shine like the northern star. And he had every intention of being the man holding the chisel.

Thirteen

Even the frigid air couldn't diminish the joy Ginger felt at sitting in the Bible meeting with the rest of the camp. They'd been pushing so hard lately, the regular Sunday meetings had been sparse for the few folks that took the time to attend. No one blamed those who stayed away. There was barely time enough for a verse and a prayer before Blake forced them to travel a full day's miles. Even the most devout among them didn't grumble about the pace and traveling on the Lord's Day. Everyone understood what was at stake if they didn't reach the Blue Mountains before the snows were too deep to allow travel. But today, not only was the train still stopped because of illness, but people needed the hope that coming together to worship afforded them.

This was a smaller, more humble crowd than had met last time. Just about every family had either lost a member or a friend. When all was said and done, thirty deaths had occurred within a few days and the entire wagon train seemed at a loss to know how to carry on. That was the main reason, Toni had confided, that Sam decided to hold a formal service this morning.

Ginger tried to ignore the angry looks that a few folks aimed at Buddy. If only they knew her brother. He was the sweetest boy anyone could hope to meet. Although one person didn't seem to blame him. Katie Caldwell sat next to him, happily sharing her Bible as Sam stood tall on the gate of Toni's wagon and delivered a sermon about God's faithfulness.

Ginger divided her attention between the looks of anger toward Buddy, Katie's infatuation, and Sam's sermon. She didn't hear a lot of it, but when he said, "With God all things are possible," she perked right up and decided to pay attention.

"He's brought us through a twister, Indians, outlaws, and now cholera." The half-Indian scout and camp preacher's voice never wavered. "We can trust God to help us fight the rest of the giants we have to face and bring us into the promised land."

Sam's voice rose with passion, igniting Ginger's faith and courage to go the rest of the journey. She fought the urge to holler *amen* with the handful of men and women that spoke out in agreement.

"How can you say he brought us through?" Tension thickened the air as Ralph Crane shot to his feet. "Answer me, half-breed."

Ginger's ire rose at the man's use of the term. But she knew he was grieving, so she decided not to call him out for it. Besides, Sam appeared to be comfortable dealing with the situation on his own.

"You're still here, aren't you?" he replied, his voice laden with sympathy.

The man's face was awash with tears as he shook his head in what appeared to be a fight for clarity. "What good is it for me to be here if my boy is gone?" He turned and shoved his finger toward Buddy. Ginger tensed, her hand going instinctively to her revolver. She fingered her pistol and sat forward, poised to take whatever action might become necessary to protect her brother. "How can he still be alive when my boy is gone?"

Buddy's face blanched, and fear shook his voice and hands, but he turned to Sam. "I'd like to know the answer to that, too, preacher."

His response seemed to throw his accuser off course. The rest of the onlookers remained silent. But Buddy wasn't finished. He stood, still facing Sam. "I never knew much about Jesus and such until I joined this camp. And I'm still a little confused why a man so good would died for someone that ain't been so good."

"Don't try to bring God into this, boy!" Ralph had recovered his voice and to Ginger's dismay, Buddy's heartfelt speech didn't seem to be having a softening affect on the grieving father. "You and that pa of yours brought the cholera to us."

That was all Ginger could take. She jumped to her feet. "Ralph, you'd best shut that trap of yours. Now, I know you're mourning your son. It's natural to want to find someone to blame, but there is no one to blame here. My brother fell off his horse from being so sick he couldn't stay in the saddle, and the scouts brought him into camp. And I'm not sorry they did! As much as you're blaming God for taking your son, I'm thanking Him for sparing Buddy."

"You are, Ginger?" Surprise widened Buddy's eyes.

Irritated, Ginger glared at him. "Don't butt in, Buddy. Of course I'm glad you're alive."

But, again, he wouldn't be deterred. "Do you really believe in God and Jesus, like these folks?"

Faced with the question, all the fire went out of Ginger. She shrugged and said simply, "Yes, I do believe. In my heart, I know we grew up in a dark place, and this place is light. Even with the troubles and hard times, there's goodness and hope among these God-fearing people. I saw that right off. I figure only someone who knows God can have that."

"But do you know Him?" Buddy pressed. "Like they do?"

Ginger's palms were dampening at the realization that she and Buddy were at the center of everyone's attention. "Why do you keep asking all these questions?"

"Because I want to know Him like the doctor does, and all these other people. They pray and really believe God is listening."

Ginger remembered not long ago she'd felt silly for speaking to God. "Well, there's no point in praying to thin air, is there?"

Toni stepped up beside her and placed an arm around her shoulders. "Do you want to answer Buddy's question?"

Ginger swallowed hard to fight back tears and all thoughts of Ralph and his accusations were pushed firmly from her mind. "If I know God?"

Toni nodded.

Yes would be a lie, but it wasn't as thought she didn't know him either. After all, she'd been coming to the meetings for some time now. She'd even prayed. In the end, she gave a shrug and answered, "I don't know."

"You can be sure today, if you want," Sam said.

Ginger had seen other people go forward and join the "family of God," as they called it. She'd silently mocked at times, had been defensive at others and walked away, but now she had no desire to do any of those things.

She glanced at Buddy to ask if he wanted to go with her, but the boy was already headed forward. Amid murmurs of praise from the wagon train members, he knelt at a make-shift altar of wood and pickle barrels and gave his life to God. Before Ginger quite knew what was happening, she started forward on wobbly legs and joined him. When she stood up fifteen minutes later, she felt her insides light up as her lungs took in a fresh breath of clean air.

Soon she was surrounded by women ready to embrace her. "Sister Ginger," they called her, eliciting an uncertain grin from her lips.

Suddenly, the crowd of women parted, and Grant stood in front of her, his handsome face split into a tender smile, his eyes moist. He didn't make a move toward her, but his arms opened. "May I?" he asked.

A laugh bubbled up from deep inside of her and left her throat as she nodded and stepped into his embrace.

From the corner of her eyes, she saw a man step toward Buddy. She tensed in Grant's arms and pulled back as she realized Ralph was face-to-face with her brother. Her blood ran cold. All she could see was Buddy, dying on the ground. Just like Clem.

Grant followed her gaze. He took her arm. "Wait," he whispered. "Look at Ralph's face. That's not anger."

The lined, weathered face was wet with tears. He shoved a book toward Buddy. "My son's Bible."

A gasp left Buddy's throat. "I don't know what to say, sir. I don't feel right takin' it from you." And yet he eyed the book like a starving man staring at a venison steak.

Ralph took a deep, broken breath. "I asked why God spared you. And now I know."

"Sir?" Buddy said, his own eyes filling with tears. He didn't even bother to wipe them away as they ran down his face.

"Samuel had known Jesus all his life. He was ready to go. You weren't. I still don't know why God would take such a good son, but I know why He brought you here and why He didn't let you die. It seems fittin' you take Samuel's Bible. That book was his pride and joy." A sad, fond smile tipped the corners of his lips. "'Bout wore it out from readin' it so much."

Finally, Buddy reached out and took the Bible. He hugged it close. "I'll treasure it, sir. I won't let it out of my sight."

"Treasure the words inside. They'll teach you how to live."

Awe filled Buddy's face. "Honest?"

"Every word is inspired by God above. I believe that. Even if I forgot it myself for a little while."

"Thank you, sir! Thank you."

Ralph sniffed back a fresh onslaught of tears, cleared his throat, clapped Buddy on the shoulder, and then turned without a word. The travelers made an aisle for him.

Ginger lifted her gaze to Grant.

His eyes were on her, and he smiled. Reaching forward, he thumbed away tears she hadn't known were there. Suddenly shy, she averted her gaze. There were still a lot of questions in her mind. Still things to confess. She knew she cared for Grant, but as she read in his eyes how much he cared for her, she couldn't muster up the same kind of optimism plainly written on his face. On the contrary, she was plagued with uncertainty. Despite her new status in the family of God, there were still a lot of secrets between them.

How on earth could they ever move past such obstacles and be together? Sam had said with God all things were possible. But how could that be, with something as impossible as this? Ginger couldn't bear for him to look at her that way. Not now. She gathered a short breath. "I have to go."

He gave a little laugh of disbelief. "What do you mean?"

"Miss Sadie is waiting for the tent. I'll be back in a few days."

She left him staring after her, and she knew he was more than likely confused. But if he knew what she did, he'd understand. She'd have to tell him soon. She only hoped he didn't hate her forever when he found out that it was her fault his beloved wife had died.

Grant stared after Ginger, shaking his head in disbelief at her abrupt exit. How could she live through such a momentous occasion and walk away as though nothing had happened? Not only that, but she had given him the first real indication that she might possibly share his feelings and might care for him. And she wanted to just leave?

Determination compelled him forward, and he was glad for all the well-wishers who slowed her flight. It gave him a chance to catch up to her before she'd gone more than a few feet.

"Ginger, wait."

A ragged breath quivered through her body as she continued to walk. "Not now, Grant."

"I can't just let you go on back, as though nothing has
happened."

She shook her head, her eyes filled with . . . sadness? How
could that be at a time like this? "I have to go. I'll be back
as soon as Miss Sadie says the men will make it. Then we'll
have to talk, but I can't yet. Please understand."

"I want to. I truly do. But those men don't deserve your
attention, Ginger. They're outlaws, thieves. Murderers."

She flinched. "You took care of Buddy when you had to
have known he was part of the outlaws band that attacked us
that day. I know you were pretending to give us the benefit
of the doubt, but only a fool wouldn't have figured it out. I
imagine Blake's going to kick us right out as soon as the cholera sickness is over, anyway."

"Well, I don't know about that. But Buddy was different.
Buddy's just a boy. Those others are full grown men and they
know exactly what they're doing. And they don't care who
they hurt."

"Some of them do, Grant," she said with earnest appeal.
"There's a fellow named Yuley. He's not much older than
I am, but in his mind, he's like Alfie Harrison. He and his
brother Cal joined Web after their parents were killed in an
Indian attack. Cal was shot and killed a few years ago, and
Yuley stays because no one has the heart to kick him out.
Most of the men are real good to him. And he doesn't know
any better. Doesn't remember a different life. He holds the

horses when the men do an inside job. But I don't believe a jury would convict someone like Yuley. So, if for no other reason, I have to go back for him. When I left, he was sick and grieving his best friend, an old timer named Dale."

As usual, when faced with Ginger's tender side, Grant didn't quite know what to say. They walked along in silence, Ginger leading the way back to her wagon.

Grant knew there was no changing her mind, but that didn't quell the frustration he felt that she was leaving just when they were beginning something important. Or something worth trying, anyway.

She shimmied up to the wagon seat before he could help her. He stood staring up, knowing his eyes reflected the fullness of his heart. "Before you go, I want to tell you something. There's a reason I don't care for outlaws."

She gave a short laugh. "Only one? There's not much to like about them in general, is there?"

He reached up and placed his hand over hers, though she held tightly to the reins. "I have more than a general reason. My reasons are personal."

Ginger's throat moved up and down as she swallowed hard. "I know, Grant."

"No. You couldn't possibly. Something terrible happened to me a few years back."

"Seven years. Next month, it will be seven years." She stared down at him, hard. "Listen to me," she said, never allowing her gaze to leave his. She spoke slowly, intently, as though attempting to reach out to his very soul. "Your wife was killed during an outlaw attack. It happened in Missouri while you were traveling by stagecoach. She was shot through the window. It was an accident. Still, she was dead, even before you carried her out of the coach and laid her on the ground."

A tingle moved up and down Grant's spine as her words played the scene over in his mind with vivid reality. *But . . .* he opened his mouth to speak, but words were impossible. His brain sought answers. Some sort of logic. He was an educated man, after all. Why couldn't he make sense of how . . . ? Then he remembered the young girl, crying over her brother only a few feet from him that day. One long braid. He heard himself expel a poof of air, as though he'd been punched in the gut. Horror plunged into his chest like a spear.

Ginger pulled her hands away from his, leaving his palm exposed to the cold air. "I'm sorry, Grant," she said in a hoarse whisper. "I'm so sorry. Please, just let me go now."

Flapping the reins, she nudged the oxen on. Grant could easily have caught up with her, but his feet remained planted where he stood, his legs paralyzed. How could he have been so blind? So stupid? There was no doubt that Web's gang of outlaws had been the ones that killed Sarah, but even faced with this horrifying reality, he couldn't muster anger. Or any emotion, really. All he felt was numb.

He paid little attention to the commotion going on at the front of the wagon train as he staggered like a drunkard back to his tent. Whatever it was, they'd have to face it without him. He simply had no more to give.

Fourteen

Ginger almost didn't recognize the outlaw camp as she pulled the reins and halted the oxen. The stench and clutter from a few days ago were gone, and instead, there seemed to be a sense of order. She grinned to herself, imagining Miss Sadie organizing the cleanup effort and demanding help from anyone able to stand on his feet.

Miss Sadie straightened up from her place bent over the fire and headed toward the wagon. Her face nearly melted in relief to see Ginger back. "Thought you'd taken down with cholera, gal. According your pa, you were so sick, the doc had to carry you to your tent. You got well might-fast. Not that I'm complaining." She grinned, but it was a tired smile. Ginger noted the shadows ringing her eyes. Now that she was back, Miss Sadie could rest a little.

"Grant says it was just a weak stomach and exhaustion." She gave a sheepish grin. "Too many smells all mixing together at once. I couldn't help it."

Miss Sadie chuckled and followed her to the back of the wagon. "Well, you're not the first person to lose a meal that way."

"I guess." Ready to put the entire incident behind her,

Ginger looked past Miss Sadie. The camp seemed deserted. "Where's Yuley?"

"Off yonder, attending to the wood."

Ginger lowered the tailboard and turned to Miss Sadie. She leaned against the wagon and gave her full attention. "Thank goodness he's pulled through."

"Yep. God looks out for those that can't look out for themselves."

"How about Mr. Harrison and Web?" She gave a short laugh. "I didn't figure Web would be much help, but I thought for sure Mr. Harrison would be working up a storm like he does around our camp."

"Who do you think cleaned up the bulk of the mess around here and set fire to the burn pile?"

Ginger gave a shrug. "I don't know. Yuley?"

"Honey, no matter how sweet Yuley is, I wouldn't hand him a flint. He'd be likely to burn down the whole camp and every tree for a mile in every direction."

"Well, then, where are Web and Mr. Harrison?"

Jerking her thumb toward the tent, Miss Sadie's eyes grew somber and she shook her head. "Charles came down with it this morning. I thought he looked a little peaked yesterday, but you never can tell for sure with a man that's not your own."

Dread bubbled in Ginger's stomach and weakened her knees. "Oh, no." She shook her head. "Poor Mr. Harrison."

"Poor Amanda Kane," Miss Sadie said with another shake of her gray head. "Charles told me they're planning to get married at Fort Boise. His main concern is that she might return to the laudanum if he doesn't pull through. She's lost so much in the last few months. Her share of sorrow. Almost more than her share." She paused, then scrutinized her. "You haven't asked about Web."

"What about him?" She frowned. "He doesn't have cholera too, does he?"

"Web's ailing, but not from cholera."

Relieved that he wasn't suffering the deadly disease, Ginger couldn't hold back the short sarcastic laugh. "Then what's he ailing from? Too much liquor and not enough sleep?"

A scowl pinched Miss Sadie's face. "You could use a little more respect when you talk about your pa, you know."

Again, Ginger couldn't keep a straight face. "If I had any for him, I might use it," she retorted. "Too bad I'm fresh out." She lowered the tailboard on the wagon and started pulling on Miss Sadie's tent. "Don't worry about Web. Just let him sleep it off, and he'll wake up ready to drink some more. Hide his bottle, or you won't get a lick of work out of him."

"It might interest you to know that he wasn't drinking. As a matter of fact, I haven't seen hide nor hair of a bottle of anything. It's a lot more serious than that."

Something in the sound of her voice made Ginger stop and pay attention. "Well, what is it then?"

"I'm not a doctor, but if I had to guess, I'd say he's suffering from a wasting disease. He's all the time doubled over and favoring his right side."

Ginger frowned, remembering. In her mind's eye, she could picture Web bending over and pressing his hand to his side, sweat beading his brow as he fought the pain. She nodded. "He gets sick from time to time, doesn't he? I'd forgotten." She squinted at Miss Sadie as she realized how sober the old woman was. "Is he dying?"

"I've seen this type of illness before, and the poor person hardly ever makes it. Sometimes they might last a good while . . . months, maybe, but after a time, they pass on."

Stunned, Ginger wasn't sure what to say. A world without Web? Granted, he didn't contribute much of anything. At least not enough to balance out the things he took, but still . . .

Miss Sadie gathered up the tent stakes. She stood with her arms full and sought Ginger's gaze. "You know what worries me the most?"

Trying to come to grips with her own feelings about Web's illness, Ginger shook her head.

"If that man breathes his last breath with his soul as black as tar, he'll burn sure as that fire over there."

"Burn?" Alarmed, Ginger's gaze shot to the burn pile at the edge of camp. Then she realized it was a spiritual matter. "Oh, you mean in hell?" The situation was hopeless. Web would never give up his wicked ways. "Oh, Miss Sadie. Web's been thieving and lying practically all his life. How's he going to give it all up in time to make it to heaven when he passes on? It'll take him a hundred years to make up for all the wrong he's done."

"He could never make up it."

"Well, then I guess there's no point in telling him what to expect when he dies." Ginger shook her head, truly sorry for Web. "I wish he'd changed his ways when he was young like I did."

Surprise lit Miss Sadie's eyes. "What are you saying?"

For some reason, Ginger felt shy about sharing her new life with Miss Sadie. She wasn't ashamed. Not by a long shot. Only, it was still new, and she felt like keeping it between her and God for a while. But now that she'd opened her trap and made Miss Sadie curious, she didn't really have a choice. She ducked her head and averted her gaze. "This morning, I went up where Sam was holding the service."

Miss Sadie expelled a breath. Her eyes glittered with unshed tears. "Land sakes, are you telling me you went to the altar and prayed for forgiveness today?"

"Yes. Buddy did, too."

Miss Sadie shook her head. "Well, if that doesn't beat all. I've pretty nearly worn my knees out praying for your soul, and God goes and draws you on a day I can't witness the blessed event." She gave a little huff. "How do you feel? Different?"

"Yes. And the same in a lot of ways."

"You're not the same. Not even a little. When Jesus comes, He makes you over. You're like a newborn baby without one little sin. Well, maybe except the crack about your pa and the whiskey earlier. You need to show more respect. The Bible says so. Even a pa like the one you have deserves the honor that comes from being a parent in the first place."

"You're making that up." Ginger couldn't even imagine. Didn't God know Web? How was she supposed to respect a liar and a thief? A man that dragged his children along while he robbed trains and stagecoaches and banks? Surely Miss Sadie was mistaken. "How could the Bible say I have to respect Web?"

"Well, it doesn't exactly mention Web by name, but it says

to honor your parents so that you don't die before your time. And if you do, things will go all right for you in your life."

Ginger released a sigh. "I don't know anything about God. How does a person ever really know Him?"

"You'll learn. I'll teach you as much as I can, but mostly it comes from reading your Bible and praying. We learn God's character as we see His word come true in our lives."

"Like what?" Ginger had thought the Bible held a lot of rules. But the way Miss Sadie spoke, her voice soft and loving, made Ginger wish she owned a Bible herself.

"For instance, the Bible says when a person is in Christ, he's a new creature, old things are passed away, like we just said, and all things are new." She demanded Ginger's gaze with her own. "How do you feel different since you asked forgiveness and made the decision to become one of God's family?"

A slow smile spread across Ginger's face. "I guess like you were sayin', I feel new. Like a different person."

"There you go. You've just come face-to-face with the heart of God. If His Word says it, you can believe it. Even if you didn't feel it, it would still be true."

The very thought made Ginger go warm all over. She'd never really known anyone that always kept his word. Even Clem had gone and died, instead of taking her and Buddy out west. Life so far had been full of disappointments. But, like a flint, something inside of Ginger sparked hope. And that hope had just grown into the smallest flicker of flame.

"The first thing I'm going to help you study is the grace of God," Miss Sadie said with a smile. "You need to understand that you can't ever make up for sins. Not with God. All you can do is repent and accept His forgiveness and believe that He won't remember them."

"How can God not remember? If He's God, He knows it all."

"He forgets because he chooses to. Right in the Bible, He says he blots out our sins for His own sake and doesn't remember them. It's the same as when you rub a bar of lye soap across a pair of old trousers and scrub until whatever it is you've gotten into comes off. It's gone. And by the time you put those trousers on again, you don't even remember the stain."

While Ginger tried to wrap her mind around this new concept, she remembered something Miss Sadie had said about Web. "That's what you mean when you said Web couldn't make up for his wickedness, either."

"No one can. Not the most blessed saintly woman or the blackest heart on earth."

"Maybe so with normal folks. But Web'll never give God a chance like I did."

"Once upon a time, there were folks who said the same thing about you, my dear."

Heat crept to Ginger's face. She cleared her throat. "Where do you want the tent?"

Miss Sadie pointed to a flat spot not far from the men's tent. "Over there."

"You sure? That seems a little close to be proper."

A good-natured smile tipped Miss Sadie's lips at Ginger's teasing tone. "With an old lady like me in your tent, it'll be plenty proper."

"With my rifle next to me it would be, anyway."

They made short work of putting up the tent. Ginger thought Miss Sadie looked mighty tired. "I take it the men are all sick now?"

"They're getting better, though. Elijah's asking for you to join him as soon as you get back."

"Asking for me?" Ginger gave a frown. "I wonder why."

Miss Sadie shrugged. "He didn't say."

"Is he in the tent?"

"Yes, but you're not going in there. He should be well enough tomorrow to sit up out here awhile."

"Fannie and Blake sent you a bearskin, so I'm going to make you a pallet inside the tent, and I think you ought to sleep for a while."

The older woman pressed her fists into the small of her back and nodded wearily. That surprised Ginger. She figured she'd have to argue for a good five minutes to get the stubborn woman to take a break.

Within a few minutes, with strict instructions that she was not to go near the men's tent, Miss Sadie collapsed onto the soft pallet Ginger had made with special care.

It felt strange, eerie even, for Ginger to be in this camp while the men lay sick in one tent and Miss Sadie, exhausted from days of giving everything she had to the sick, in another. Ginger unhitched the oxen. After hobbling them, she wandered to the campfire and lifted the coffeepot, glad that there was at least a full cup left, even if it was the bottom of the pot. Alone, she felt at a loss. The pot was full of the soup and another of stew, so there was no need to cook. She felt faintly disappointed. Cooking was one of the few domestic chores where she excelled. She'd been doing all the cooking for Web's gang since she was thirteen years old. Well, Miss Sadie would be wanting coffee when she woke later, so Ginger could at least get some to boiling.

Filling the dipper with water from the bucket next to the fire, she slowly filled up the pot, barely paying any mind to the task at hand. Her thoughts turned to the conversation she'd had with Miss Sadie. If the woman was right, then God didn't remember that Ginger had joined the wagon train bent on revenge against Grant. The problem was that *she* remembered. And Grant had a right to know. He couldn't go on having ideas that he might want to court her and most likely marry her, when Ginger knew it would never be possible. Even if she loved him as much as she'd once hated him, it still wouldn't work.

Especially once he discovered who had provided the decoy that day. She had stood in the road, flagged down the stagecoach and had cowered behind a tree until she'd seen her brother, Clem, shot from his horse.

No. God might not remember it, but Ginger did. And once Grant became aware of her place in his wife's death, he'd never love her again.

But that was a chance she'd have to take. She wouldn't start out her new life by holding onto a lie. She just couldn't.

Thankfully, there was no time for her to mull it over any more, because Yuley crashed through the perimeter trees, his arms filled with a load of wood. He stumbled under the weight and almost dropped his burden. Ginger hopped up and hurried to help him. His eyes were still dark and sunken in, much like Buddy's, but clearly, his strength was returning. He grinned broadly, showing only a few teeth left in his mouth. "I'm glad to see you, Miss Ginger!"

"I'm glad to see you up and about, Yuley. How you feeling?"

"Better. I thought I was going to die like Dale did. You want to see where we buried him? You never got to say goodbye."

That was just about the last thing Ginger wanted to do. She'd seen enough death. Dale would have to do without her. "I'll say goodbye another time. Right now, I have to get the fire built back up so that we can get that soup boiling again."

His expression drooped. "I don't much like that soup, Miss Ginger. I'm fixin' to go to the river and catch us some fish."

"There's some stew."

He wrinkled his nose. "I don't much care for it, neither. Ate it for breakfast."

"It's kind of cold to be fishing. You think they'll bite?"

"Sure they will!"

"All right, Yuley," she said, dropping the wood to the ground by the fire. "I'll tell you what: if you catch some fish and clean it by the river, I'll cook it for your supper." She nodded toward the pot of stew. "But if you don't catch any, you have to have a bowl of that stew. You need to keep up your strength."

He frowned, clearly weighing his odds. Then he nodded. "Thank you, Miss Ginger. I'll do it." He started to dash off, then turned back to her. He closed the distance between them in a few lanky strides. "Forget something, Yuley?"

"I got to tell you something."

"What is it, Yuley?"

"I can't be an outlaw no more."

"You can't?" Ginger held back the smile lurking at the

corners of her lips. The thought of Yuley as an outlaw was just silly.

"Miss Sadie says it ain't right."

Ginger took a breath and released it in a cloud of frigid air. Land sakes, Miss Sadie ought not to say things like that, right in the midst of outlaws. She could get herself hurt. Or worse, if she angered someone like Lane. He'd put a bullet into her without thinking twice. "I suppose it's not right, but no one is going to hold it against you."

"I just want to do what's right. Like Miss Sadie."

How could she encourage him to stay with this band of thugs if she herself had no intention of staying? "It's okay, Yuley. You don't have to be an outlaw anymore if you don't want to." And then an idea hit her that was so ridiculous in its simplicity that she had no idea if it would work or not. "How would you like to go to Oregon with me?"

"I think I'd like that fine." A slow grin spread across his face and before she knew what was happening, he swooped her up into a tight hug that lifted her clean off her feet. "You won't change your mind will you?"

"Of course not. I want you to come with me and Buddy. It'll be like having two brothers again."

"That'd be good. I ain't never had a sister."

"Well, now you will. What about those fish? If you don't hurry up, they're going to think you don't want a fish dinner, and they'll all swim away."

"Aw, Miss Ginger, you're teasin' me."

Chuckling, he moved off toward the saddlebag that held all of his belongings, including his fishing tackle. Walking toward the river, he turned and gave her a hardy wave.

Ginger grinned and shook her head, staring after him. She heard footsteps behind her and turned to find Web coming. He stopped when he reached a rough-hewn bench. Sweat dotted his forehead, despite the frigid air. Miss Sadie was right. Sickness had somehow caught Web, and if he didn't do something about it fast, he'd be swallowed up in death.

Web nodded toward Yuley. "You got a special way with him, you know. Always did."

She shrugged. "Yuley's a good boy."

"I heard what you said to him about going to Oregon with you and Buddy."

Ginger raised her chin. "That's right. He wants to stop riding with you, because he doesn't feel right about it anymore. I've seen you let men walk out of the gang before with no hard feelings. Surely you won't stop Yuley."

He pursed his lips and gave a slow, thoughtful nod. "*He* can go if he wants. I only kept him around for his brother's sake, anyhow."

Something in the way he stressed *he* wrapped a tight fist of dread around Ginger's gut. "But not me or Buddy?"

"Like I said, we got one more job to do; then I'll let you go."

Summoning courage she didn't even know if she possessed, she stared into Web's eyes. "I'm not doing any jobs. We agreed after Clem died that I didn't have to help after that. I can't steal anymore than I could kill Grant. I'm not the same as I used to be. I've been around folks that work hard for a living. Folks that care about each other. And I like them. I'm not stealing from them."

"Look, I know I didn't give you the chance to be around decent folks much. And maybe I was wrong for that."

Anytime Web admitted to any wrongdoing, he was probably lying through his teeth. He didn't have a sincere bone in his body and everyone knew it. She opened her mouth to tell him as much, but Miss Sadie's words came back to her in a flash. She swallowed her skepticism and tried to wipe the disbelief from her face. "Well, I'll be around decent folks from now on. And so will Buddy. So don't fret about it."

"Look, girl." His graying eyebrows shoved together in a deep frown. "You're gonna have to do what I say, or you might get into more trouble than you bargained for."

"Like being forced to marry the likes of Lane Conner?"

"You know about that?"

"Lane told me." She gave him a pointed look. "And he kissed me, against my will and threatened to do more than that."

Anger flashed in his eyes again. This time directed toward Lane.

"Lane knows I'm sick. I'm tryin' to make sure you're looked after when I'm gone."

"Miss Sadie told me about that, Web. I'm truly sorry you're not well, but I can't marry Lane. I can hardly tolerate ten minutes anywhere near him. Besides, if I married Lane, I'd probably have to shoot him within a year."

"Let me tell you about the job."

"Not that I have a choice."

"Elijah's been writing letters to a man in California. A man that struck it rich in the gold mines."

"I don't know what you're getting at, Web."

"Well, hush up and listen, and you will."

Same old Web.

"He wrote some real fancy, pretty letters, if you know what I mean."

"What for?" Ginger's mind tried to wrap around the point Web was trying to make, but just why Elijah would write fancy, pretty letters to a man in California didn't make any sense whatsoever. Unless . . . Ginger shoved to her feet. "Do you mean Elijah answered a rich man's advertisement for a wife?"

His face brightened. "I always said you was a bright girl."

"It appears I'm the only bright one around here," she mumbled. "That's about the dumbest idea I've ever heard. How did you plan on . . ." And then she knew. "Elijah pretended to be me, didn't he?"

"That's right. Now you're catchin' on." He looked so pleased with himself, Ginger realized this must have been his bright idea in the first place. "Tell me about the plan."

Reaching into his pocket, Web drew out a fistful of letters. Ginger took the dirty envelopes. "I figure Elijah's about dead. I took these from his bag."

Ginger gave the handful a cursory glance and sniffed. "Letters from the man in California, I take it."

"Yep." Web beamed with pride. "You read them letters and see what I mean. I need you to meet him, and we'll take it from there."

"I don't see how my meeting him will give you the opportunity to rob him. For this big a job, you have something more in mind. This is a little too easy."

He gave a sigh of resignation. "Okay. You might have to marry him. But it'd only be for a little while."

Horror filled Ginger. "What? Marry him! Web, are you crazy? First you want me to marry Lane; now you want me to marry this fellow in California? Do you want me to live with them both at the same time?"

Instead of boxing her ears for her impertinence, Web grinned, showing a mouthful of mostly missing teeth. "Feisty, aren't ya? After we get his money, we'll leave California, and you won't have nothing to worry about."

"I'd still be married."

"Only if you look at it that way. That's up to you."

"It's the way it would be, Web. No matter how I look at it. God would see me as married to that man. You really want to force me to do that, just so you can line your pockets?"

"You know I don't cotton to talk about God." A dangerous glint flickered in his eyes. A sign Ginger recognized as Web nearing the end of his patience. "Just read those letters. You just might like the man's pretty words."

"How would you know what they say?"

"Elijah read 'em to us."

"But how did they get back and forth so quick?"

Clearly at the end of his patience, Web struggled to his feet and towered over her. "I ain't askin', Ginger. If you want to leave us, this is your chance. You do one job for us, and you, Buddy, and Yuley are free to go. If you don't . . . well, let's just say, you won't be goin' anywhere."

"You're threatening your own daughter?"

"I don't want to. But you forced me to it. Now you simmer

down and do as you're told, and before long, you'll be free."

He moved away, and Ginger faced her first test as the new person she'd become. The opportunity to gain her freedom or staying true to the new feelings of truth and goodness inside.

Was there anything in the Bible about how to get out of this mess? If only she could ask Miss Sadie about it. A sigh escaped her as she sat on the bench and opened the first letter.

Elijah,

I'm grateful you've reached Missouri and have joined up with Web. Be careful, my pa may not have learnin' but he's smart in the ways of man. He won't be easy to fool. The most important thing is not to make him suspicious. If he gets wind of who you really are, he'll kill you and that'll be the end of our plans for Ginger . . .

Ginger frowned and reread the first part of the letter. Clearly, Elijah had been pulling a job of his own. One that had nothing to do with a man in California. Indignation shot through her. How dare he? Web wouldn't know any better.

A chill scurried up her spine and she shuddered. Her eyes skimmed the rest of the letter, and when she reached the last words, a gasp tore through her throat.

It won't be too much longer before I'll be able to join them. Thank you again, my friend.

God Bless and keep you,
Clem

Fifteen

Grant had that unsettling feeling someone was watching him even before he opened his eyes and confirmed the truth. He sat up on his pallet and came face-to-face with Buddy Freeman.

He frowned through a pounding headache. "Buddy? What are you doing?"

The boy ducked his head. "Mr. Tanner asked me to come find you. I hated to wake you up. But you've been sleeping since the church meeting this morning and it's almost suppertime."

"What's the problem?"

"Soldiers from Fort Boise rode in a couple of hours ago."

"So why call for the doctor? Are they sick?"

Buddy shrugged. "I don't know, sir."

"All right," Grant said, standing. He tried to shake off the clutter in his brain. Four hours wasn't enough sleep when it was all he'd had per night for over a week. What he wouldn't give to lie down again and sleep for a solid twelve hours. He knew he'd feel like a new man. He released a breath. But a person didn't ignore the wagon master when he called. So he ignored the ache in his muscles, the queasiness of his stomach, and the pain in his head, and inched his way to the tent flap, fighting dizziness.

"Doctor Kelley? Are you feeling okay?"

A spasm seized his gut. "I'm fine," he gasped out. But he wasn't. So much for the disease coming to an abrupt end. The worst thing for a doctor was coming down with his patients' disease and being unable to help those who still needed him. "Buddy, please ask Mrs. Kane to come see me. And tell Blake I'm not going to be able to meet with him." He took hold of Buddy's arm just before he could dash out to do what he'd been told. "Don't mention anything about sickness in front of the soldiers. We don't want to risk them getting jittery about the wagon train and not allowing us to winter at the fort even after cholera is over."

Another wave of dizziness swept over him. He back-tracked to his pallet and fell across the blankets, fighting hard to keep from retching. "Buddy, hand me the black bag and that bucket."

The boy's eyes were wide as he brought the items. He opened the bag without being told and lifted out the quinine. "Is this what you're wanting?"

"Yes. Thanks. Please, go get Amanda Kane and tell Blake I'm not coming."

Grant took a dose of quinine and prayed it would begin to work quickly. One thing was for certain—by tomorrow night, he would either be dead or getting better. That was the nature of cholera. It came on suddenly and killed quickly and violently. Grant had seen the killer strike more times than he cared to count. Only now it was personal. He was the one lying sick retching violently, and soon it would be even worse and he wouldn't be able to get off his mat. As a matter of fact, even now, he felt the need to stay put. His limbs were shaky and weak and he shivered under his blanket, hands and feet freezing as though he were walking barefoot in those snow-covered mountains to the west.

All he wanted to do was sleep. Then he wouldn't feel so bad. If he could lose consciousness for a few hours and allow the quinine a chance to go to work for him, maybe he'd wake up on his way to becoming well again.

Proper or no, Ginger slammed into the men's tent, letter in hand. "Elijah!" she hollered. "Wake up, you varmint and tell me what this means."

Greely, one of the lucky men that made it through the sickness, sat up. "Shut your trap, Ginger. We need our rest."

"It's all right." Elijah sat up, wrapping his blanket around his rail-thin shoulders. Ginger nearly gasped at his appearance. How could a man be reduced from vibrant and vital to a skeleton so quickly?

"I have to talk to you about these letters." She shoved them toward him but kept all three firmly clutched in her hands.

Greeley and Ames laughed. Sickness sure hadn't scared the meanness out of them.

"Web finally let you in on the new plan, huh?" Ames asked.

Elijah slowly shoved to his feet and clutched her arm. "Let's go outside."

Glaring, Ginger jerked away with such force, Elijah tee-tered between his toes and heels and almost fell. She grabbed onto his arm. "You okay?"

"Just a little dizzy." His eyes pleaded, and he shifted his gaze quickly between the other men and Ginger, as though trying to convey something private. "Can we go out and talk about those letters?"

Intrigued, Ginger nodded and they stepped outside, Elijah trembling and moving slowly. Ginger shook, as well, but from anticipation. What on earth was going on?

Elijah took Ginger by the elbow and led her to the bench Yuley had constructed. A puff of air left his lungs as he dropped to the seat. "I take it you've read the letters?"

Tears blurred Ginger's vision as she nodded. "What does this mean?"

Tenderly he took her hand and cradled it between his clammy palms. "Clem and I were in prison together."

All of Ginger's strength left her and she didn't even have the energy to pull her hand free, which is what instinct dic-tated. "But I saw him die seven years ago."

"No. He was wounded badly, but there was a doctor on the stagecoach that removed the bullet and stopped the bleeding. Your brother said the Marshal aboard wanted to leave him, but the doc refused to go without him, so they loaded him into the stage and took him back to the nearest town."

"I just can't believe it. Then why didn't he get in touch?"

"The way your pa moves around, he knew a letter would never reach you. Besides, he thought it best if Web thought he was dead. He wanted to leave the gang and plans to stay dead, as far as your pa is concerned."

Ginger's head swam as her brain fought to catch up. "Where is he?"

"He's still in prison in St. Louis. He's set to get out in a few months and plans to meet up with you and Buddy in Oregon. I was supposed to come find you."

"But when you found Web, I wasn't with the gang."

"Yes. The only way I could find out where you were without raising Web's suspicion was to insinuate I knew a rich man who was looking for a wife."

Amused, Ginger couldn't help a short laugh. "What did you plan to do once you found me? Come up with a fake rich man from California?"

"When we get to Fort Boise, I planned to fake a telegram to your so-called intended and have him break off the engagement."

"The cad! He's going to break my heart?"

Elijah's blue eyes twinkled, and he laughed. "Well, he's found someone else. The true love of his life. What do you expect him to do?"

"Ah, well, I suppose I'll live through the humiliation." She sent him a conspiratorial grin. "Especially if I have the joy of being reunited with my long-lost brother instead."

"I think that can be arranged."

Ginger felt like she was a little girl all over again as a giddy joy bubbled up inside of her. "When can I see him?"

"He's set for release in February."

"Well, that's too long to wait. I'm going to see him. Where in St. Louis? What's the name of the prison?"

Shaking his head, Elijah squeezed her hand. "He doesn't want you anywhere near that place."

"But . . ."

Elijah raised his other hand. "Trust me. He's right. But he'll come and find you. From the looks of things, you'll be spending the winter at Fort Boise. One telegram, and he can come find you before the wagon train pulls out again in the spring."

Ginger wanted to protest. Her heart raced. She hadn't seen her brother in seven years and had no intention of waiting another six months to see him. But something in Elijah's eyes begged her to respect Clem's wishes and wait for him to come to her.

The sound of horses' hooves interrupted the conversation. Ginger tensed as Lane rode into camp, along with the men who had left camp during the cholera outbreak. Lane dismounted and stared from her to Elijah. His lip curled into a sneer. "Well, ain't this just cozy? Is there somethin' you two need to tell me? After all, she's my girl." He sent a suggestive wink that made Ginger's skin crawl. "Ain't ya, honey?"

"Maybe if I was blind and soft in the head."

Laughter rumbled through the group of men. "She told you, Conners," Greely called. Ginger snapped her gaze around to the men's tent. All of the men except for Charles Harrison stood outside, presumably to greet their fellow outlaws. They were a pale, weak looking group of men, but Ginger couldn't help but be glad they were going to make it. Only three had died. Much fewer than the wagon train casualties.

Lane's eyes narrowed dangerously. "Shut up," he growled.

He turned to Elijah. "You best get away from her before I finish what the cholera started."

Elijah stood slowly and raised his hand, palm forward. "Take it easy. We're just talking."

"Besides," Ginger said, shooting up next to him. "How many times do I have to tell you I'm not going to marry you, Lane? I don't want to hurt your feelings, but I don't care what Web promised you. I'm not going to marry you—now or ever."

In a flash, Lane reached out and grabbed her arm. Elijah stepped forward. "Let go of her."

"Better do as you're told, Lane." Web's voice of authority rang through the air. "What have I told you about grabbing my daughter?"

Ginger couldn't help but note the irony of the situation. "And yet you're the one that promised me to this idiot. And you want to practically sell me to a man in California for your cut of a gold mine."

"I'm trying to help you, girl," Web said.

Fighting against the anger, Ginger bit back a retort. "And I appreciate it," she said.

"Well, act like it then," Web gasped out. "I come to find Miss Sadie. Harrison's bad off."

"Miss Sadie's sleeping. I'll see to him."

"You ain't nursin' no other men," Lane said.

Ginger sneered and slid past him. "He's an old man. And he needs my help." She glanced at Web. "Will you go back in there and let Mr. Harrison know I'll be there in just a minute? Elijah, you should go back to bed."

Elijah shook his head. "I think I'll go have a bath."

"Are you crazy?" Ginger stared into his clouded eyes. Clearly he needed to be back in the tent, napping. "You can't dip in that freezing cold water. You'll end up with pneumonia!"

He smiled gently. "I'll be fine. I promise."

"Look, are you coming or not?" Web called from the tent.

"Hold your horses, Web!"

She turned back to Elijah. "Fine. Get pneumonia. See if I care." She stomped to the fire and ladled a bowl of onion soup then stomped back to the men's tent.

The men had dispersed, and only Web and Charles remained. Ginger's eyes widened at the sight of poor Mr. Harrison. His face was pale, his cheeks sunken, eyes dark. He looked closer to death than life. "Mr. Harrison," she said softly. "I'm here to give you some soup. Web's going to help you sit up." She nodded to Web, and he moved to Mr. Harrison's side and lifted his shoulders. Ginger scooped a spoonful and placed it on his lips. He moaned and turned his head. "I can't."

"If you don't take this, it can't kill the cholera."

"I'm going to die anyway," Mr. Harrison said. He turned to Web. "Let me lay down."

"Don't do it, Web." Ginger lifted another spoonful to Mr. Harrison's lips and glared at him. "Didn't you hear me?"

Mr. Harrison swallowed down the liquid but waved away the next spoonful. He pushed back and finally, Ginger nodded to Web. "Let him lay down for a minute."

"I need to talk to you both," Mr. Harrison said. He turned to Web. "I need you to do something for me, and Ginger is the witness."

Mercy, this sounded like the kind of speech a person

made when they knew they weren't long for this world. But they could save Mr. Harrison. "Listen," Ginger said. "You're a couple of days behind the other men in getting cholera. But almost all of the others have made it just fine. Eat the soup. You'll be well in no time."

Shaking his head, Mr. Harrison took her hand. "I have to say this, just in case."

Ginger glanced up at Web. His eyes glittered a little too brightly for someone sitting at a dying man's bedside. This just seemed like a bad idea.

"I don't think you should do this."

Web glared her to silence. "If Charles wants to talk, you ought to let him. A man knows what he needs to do at a time like this."

She wanted to call him out. To urge Mr. Harrison to keep quiet and not say anything about his money. But the look in Web's eyes told her she'd better not, and Ginger cowered.

"This may come as a shock to you," Mr. Harrison began, his voice shaky, weak. "I am a very rich man."

"You are?" Web's voice sounded so insincere Ginger wanted to hit him. But Mr. Harrison was too weak to notice.

"Yes. I brought most of it with me."

"Without anyone knowing? You could have been robbed."

Clenching her fists, Ginger clamped her jaw shut to keep from revealing Web's appalling secret.

Charles looked at Web. "I never knew I'd fall in love again after my wife died. But I did. I hate to put this on you, but I need you to see to it that my children receive two-thirds of my money, and Amanda gets the rest."

"Sure, sure," Web said. "Just tell me where it's at, and I'll be happy to see to it for ya."

"Web . . ."

"Let Charles talk," Web growled. He turned to Mr. Harrison, his voice too eager. "You were about to tell us where you hid the money."

"Swear to me," Mr. Harrison said. "Swear that you'll make sure Amanda gets one-third of the money."

Web nodded. "Yes, I swear. She'll get her share."

"I created a false bottom in my wagon. Within the false bottom, there are two hidden compartments. One at the front and one at the back of the wagon."

The light in Web's eyes brightened, and he nodded. Ginger couldn't believe it. Web was impressed. "I never would have thought of that."

Mr. Harrison shrugged, oblivious to the reason for Web's sudden respect.

Inwardly, Ginger cringed. Web would easily have spotted the false bottom, but he never would have thought to look for secret compartments. Why did Mr. Harrison have to be such a fool when it came to trusting people? But what more could one expect from a man who took an interest in Amanda Kane, even before she stopped taking laudanum? He trusted, believed in people. The main problem was that the wagon was right here. Mr. Harrison and Web had brought the supplies in it. Poor Mr. Harrison.

"Mr. Harrison," Ginger said. "I'll do my best to see to it that Amanda and the children will receive their share of the money. *If* you don't pull through this. Which you won't, if you don't take the soup."

"I can't."

"What do you think will happen to Alfie if you die? That poor boy barely understands that he'll never see his ma again. Who will take care of him?"

Tears sprang to Mr. Harrison's eyes and Ginger knew she was getting to him. "And Belinda. What's a thirteen-year-old girl going to do without a ma or pa?"

"Don't you worry none about that," Web broke in. "I'll take both of them kids. I'll take care of them like they was my own young'uns."

Ginger noted the alarm in Mr. Harrison's eyes and took the opportunity to try to press her point. "No one can take care of them the way you can, Mr. Harrison. They need you to try."

The tears glistening in his eyes began to trail down sides of his head and drop onto the blanket. He nodded.

"Web," Ginger said. "Could you help him up?"

Web scowled and gave a grudging nod. Ginger began spooning the soup into Mr. Harrison's mouth, praying that he'd get better before Web had a chance to clean out that false bottom.

Sixteen

Grant had never felt so weak in his life. He knew there was no point in even trying to stand; he'd only crash to the ground. Even the idea of opening his eyes seemed too much of an effort. He vaguely remembered the retching and other things equally revolting. His stomach no longer roiled and rolled. His heart lifted a little. He would live.

"Doc?"

He recognized Buddy's voice and turned his head toward the sound, debating whether or not he wanted to attempt to open his eyes and face the pain a flash of light would bring.

"How long have I been sick?"

"Two days." Buddy's voice rose with relief. "Amanda said once you made it past the first twenty-four hours, you'd live."

"Lucky me." He truly was grateful, but the pain in his head . . .

"Doctors always make the worst patients, they say."

Grant's eyes flew open at the sound of Blake's voice. He groaned as the light rammed into his eyes like heavy fists.

"How are you feeling?" Blake asked.

Grant offered a weak smile. "Sick."

"Understandable."

"Why are you watching me sleep?"

"Buddy said you've been stirring for the last hour. I needed to speak with you as soon as possible. I know it's not the best time, but it's necessary."

"What is it?"

"Sunday a few soldiers arrived from Fort Boise. They heard we had cholera from their Indian scouts and warned us to stay away from the fort."

"It's a fearsome disease. I can't say I blame them."

"That may be, but we have to find someplace to hole up for the winter. We need the protection of the fort if we stay in these parts."

"You've made up your mind, then?"

Blake gave a nod, his lips set in a grim line. "We'll have some trouble out of a few of the men. I'm anticipating that. But it's the smartest thing to do. According to the soldiers, the snow is heavy this year. With four hundred miles to go, it would be folly to even attempt to get over the Blue Mountains."

"Most of the folks trust you to do what's right. None of the setbacks have been your fault."

Blake's jaw twitched as he clamped down on his back teeth, something he did when trying to control his emotions. Grant figured he'd best change the subject for now.

"What did you want me to say to the soldiers?"

"You'll need to speak to the captain and let him know there's no danger of cholera anymore. Explain it to him in doctor talk so he knows you're a real doctor."

Lifting himself, Grant rested on his elbow. His head swam with the sudden movement, and he closed his eyes until the spell passed. "How many new cases have occurred since I took sick?"

"None," Buddy said. "Everyone's getting better. Kip went fishing with me yesterday."

Grant smiled at the lad. "Catch anything?"

"Naw. Too cold. But we shot a couple of rabbits on the way back from the river."

"Well, that's something, isn't it?"

"Yes sir. Mrs. Kane roasted them over the fire. They were right tasty."

"Glad to hear it." Now that he looked closer, he could see that Buddy's face, though still thin, no longer had that sunken in appearance. He turned to Blake. "If I've been sick three days and I was the last one to come down with cholera, then it's over."

"You sure? You thought that before you got sick."

"I'm sure."

Relief washed across Blake's face. "As soon as you're strong enough to ride, we need to go to the fort so you can reassure the captain. They want to hear it from the doctor."

"The word of a wagon master isn't good enough for the captain?"

Blake gave a chuckle. "Maybe he's known too many wagon masters that don't tell the truth."

Grant felt his strength winding down. He took a deep, shaky breath. "I should be strong enough in a couple of days."

"That's good. I'll send Two Feathers on to let them know

that we'll be ready to rendezvous in a couple of days and the wagon train can move out again in three days' time."

"Sounds good." He closed his eyes and lowered himself back to the pallet. "Ginger and Miss Sadie back yet?"

The hesitation in the tent spoke loudly, and Grant opened his eyes once more, staring at Blake. "Well?"

Blake shook his head. "Not yet."

"Has anyone gone to check on them?"

A scowl marred Blake's face. "We're trying to recover from this illness. Too many men are just now regaining their strength. I didn't want to risk any kind of relapse."

"What about Web and Mr. Harrison?"

Blake shook his head.

"Blake, you know what Web is!" Grant felt the panic rising. "We have to go get them. We can't just leave Miss Sadie and Ginger and Mr. Harrison to their mercy."

"I already promised Fannie and Toni that we'd send a few men after them tomorrow, if they aren't back by then."

"Good." With his energy spent, Grant could do little more than utter the word as he closed his eyes. He hated the feeling of helplessness. The weakness. What if Ginger needed him, and he wasn't there to help her? Ginger . . . now he remembered the little girl who had been there the day his Sarah had died. His muddy memory took him back to that awful day, but his heart only saw a young girl's tears for her brother and he knew he couldn't blame her. Even now, he could only love her.

Ginger woke up with a filthy hand clasped over her mouth. "Get up, gal."

"Web? What are you doing?"

"Time to leave."

Disappointment squeezed at her. After two days she'd hoped Web had changed his mind. "Listen, Web, you don't have to do this. Don't take Mr. Harrison's money. He trusted you. Do you know what an honor it was for a man like that to trust you with his children's future?"

"Harrison's an idiot. And you know what they say."

"Yes," she said dully. "A fool and his money are soon parted."

"That's right."

"Mr. Harrison isn't a fool, Web. He's just a good man who never would have guessed that the man he's befriended would rob him. Especially when no one else in the wagon train would give you the time of day once they found out Buddy brought cholera and you're his pa."

"That was his mistake."

There was obviously no talking him out of it. "Where are we going?"

"California. Where do you figure?"

Ginger's heart rose with a thought. "Web, why do you need to take Mr. Harrison's money when you have all that man's gold waiting for you?"

"What's wrong with taking both?"

The question almost made her laugh with its utter ridiculousness. What, indeed, could be wrong with taking Mr. Harrison's money and then moving on to that poor man in California—the one that didn't actually exist?

Elijah had left camp the day after telling her about Clem, so once again she was on her own. But she had no intention of sitting back while Web took Mr. Harrison's money. Nor would she go to California and risk missing out on Clem when he got out of prison.

"I'm not helping you take Mr. Harrison's money."

"We already got it." He yanked hard and lifted her to her feet, then he grunted as though the effort caused him pain.

"Web. Don't you want to take it easy? Why live out the rest of your days the same way you always lived?"

"What are you sayin' to me?"

"You can be better than this. You have goodness in you, Web. I know that. I've seen how you've taken care of Yuley all these years. You could make a whole new start. The folks in the wagon train . . . they don't know any better. They don't know what you've been in the past. You can have a second chance. Just forget about Mr. Harrison's money and join the wagon train. You can live in Oregon with Buddy and Yuley and me." She stopped herself short of saying, "And Clem."

"What are you talking about?" Web scowled, staring at her as though she'd suddenly gone soft in the head. "We been plannin' this Harrison robbery for months. Why would we give it up now? There's thousands of dollars in that locked box. Shoot, gal, we can buy us a whole new life with that."

Her heart nearly stopped. Thousands? She'd never seen more than fifty dollars at one time in her whole life. No wonder Mr. Harrison was so concerned that his children end up with it. He'd pulled through—was getting stronger. He'd most likely be ready to go back to the wagon train today.

Yuley adored him and the feeling seemed to be mutual, as they'd spent the last couple of days reading the Bible and discussing things that confused Yuley—which was practically everything. Ginger couldn't help but suspect Mr. Harrison's attachment to the slow-minded young man had a lot to do with his missing Alfie.

Ginger glanced over at Miss Sadie, sleeping peacefully on the other side of their tent. Why hadn't the old dowager awakened? For a split second, fear gripped her. Surely Web hadn't killed her in her sleep?

Ginger was about to call out when the woman's chest rose and fell in sleep. Relief filled her. She realized how close she'd almost come to causing Miss Sadie's death. If she woke up, Web would have no choice but to silence her. Still, it seemed odd that Miss Sadie could have slept through their conversation.

Perhaps the older woman was just exhausted from the days and days of nursing and cooking. But she'd always been a light sleeper. The slightest noise in the tent next door had pulled her from sleep and sent her rushing over to make sure one of the men didn't need her help. Ginger fought to keep from smiling to herself. Only one explanation made any sense. Miss Sadie was faking it.

Web grabbed her moccasins and held them out to her. "You can put these on after you get outside. Let's go."

The horses were saddled and ready to go by the time they got outside and Ginger slipped on her calf-high moccasins.

"It's about time," Lane hissed.

"Shut up, Lane," Ginger shot back. "Don't wake up Miss Sadie and Mr. Harrison."

Taking one of the torches that lit the camp, he rode back to Mr. Harrison's wagon and tossed it into the back.

"What do you think you're doing, you big idiot?" Reacting on instinct, Ginger sprinted to the wagon and jumped into the wagon bed. She tossed the torch into the dirt. Then she stamped out the small flames. Thankfully there was minimal damage. She glared toward Web. "Are you going to leave them stranded? Miss Sadie saved ~~the~~ your lives. Is this how you thank her?"

At least Ames and Greely had the good grace to avert their gazes and look ashamed. "Leave it alone," Ames said. "Ginger's right. We can't leave them without a way to get back to their own camp."

"But what about Buddy?" Ginger asked.

"You said yourself he wants to go to Oregon. We don't need him for this job. We finish up here, and by this time next year, the two of you should be in Oregon together."

And Clem. Her heart jumped at the thought of seeing her brother again.

And Yuley. Where was he?

Web seemed to read her mind as her gaze sifted through the riders trying to find him. "He's sleeping in the tent with Charles," Web said. "Didn't see no need to wake him up when he don't want to ride with us anymore. Get mounted up and let's go."

Ginger mounted an unfamiliar horse, wishing for her own mare. They rode out of camp, and Ginger's heart sank as reality hit her with as much force as the icy air.

Where had Elijah gone? She'd thought at least she'd have someone to help her. Now she had only two chances to get out of this: her own wits and God. Her own wits had never served her all that well, so she was glad that this time, God was on her side.

Seventeen

Grant wiped the soap from his face and tried to ignore the burning skin from where he'd just shaved off a week's worth of growth. He had not taken time to shave since cholera struck. He and Blake were due to rendezvous with the captain of Fort Boise in a couple of hours. They'd meet at a set point far enough from the fort so that they didn't accidentally infect anyone.

He dumped out his soapy, bristly water just as a wagon rolled into camp. Grant's heart jumped. It must be Miss Sadie and Ginger. He walked toward Miss Sadie's campsite. Blake had insisted that no one try to move into that spot. Miss Sadie would have had a conniption fit if anyone had dared.

Feeling more light-hearted and relieved than he had in days, he walked toward the wagon. As he drew close, he realized Ginger wasn't in the wagon. Miss Sadie reined in the oxen and nodded grimly to Grant as he offered her assistance down from the wagon. "Where is she?" he asked.

"Gone," Miss Sadie said flatly.

"What do you mean, gone?"

She shook her head wearily. "It's not her fault. Web didn't give her much of a choice. They rode out during the night."

"Web just left Buddy?"

"It appears so." She jerked her thumb toward the man in the wagon. "This is Yuley. He gave his heart to Christ and refused to be an outlaw anymore." She leaned in close and dropped her voice. "In many ways, he's a lot like Alfie, if you get my meaning."

Grant nodded.

A glad cry lifted to Grant's ears, and he turned to see Amanda Kane running toward them. "Charles!" she called. "Thank God. Oh, thank God you're all right."

He slowly climbed down from the wagon seat, rail thin and visibly weak, and Amanda fell into his arms. "It's all gone," he said. "I'm so sorry. Everything is gone."

Amanda pulled back. "What do you mean?"

"All the money. Everything. I was a fool, Amanda. I thought I was doing the right thing . . . providing for you and my children. I told Web about the money in the false wagon bottom. He took it. Every last penny."

"I'm so sorry, Charles," Amanda pulled him back into her arms. "It's all right. You started with nothing and built yourself a savings. You'll do it again. With God's help, you'll do it, but even if you don't, we'll start off the same as our friends here. Land, seeds, hard work. We'll make it just fine."

Mr. Harrison palmed her cheek and pressed a kiss to her forehead. "You're right, my dear. You're so right. We have so much to be grateful for. We're all still alive."

Amanda put her hand on his and offered a soft smile. "Let's go see the children. They've been worried."

Mr. Harrison hung back for a second. "Amanda, I want you to meet Yuley. He'll be staying with me for a while."

The young man turned a shade of red Grant hadn't seen before, and he grinned, ducking a little but keeping his eyes upward on Amanda's pretty face. "Pleased to meet ya, ma'am."

Amanda walked to the back of the wagon and offered her hand. Yuley wiped his palm on his filthy trousers and then clasped her hand.

"Would you like to come meet Mr. Harrison's children?"

"I'd be pleased to."

Grant watched them go then turned back to Miss Sadie. "I take it Charles was sick?"

"Nearly didn't make it." She scrutinized him. "Looks like you took down with it, too."

"For a couple of days. I'm much better, though."

"Charles was the sickest I've seen anyone that didn't die. I thought for sure he was going to meet his maker. So did he." She shook her head, and her eyes narrowed. "That's why he lost his money. He trusted Web. When he thought he would die within the day, Charles confided in that varmint where the money was and that he wanted it given to Amanda and his children. Ginger told me Web was all too eager."

"You say Ginger didn't want to go with them?"

"Of course she didn't." Miss Sadie stared at him. "She's a new person, Grant. She'll make a fine Christian woman. I heard Web telling her they were going to California to rob some rich man of his gold mine."

"Then I'm going after them."

"You can't go alone. There are at least nine men, and they're all counting on Ginger's help to do this other robbery in California. They're not going to let her go without a fight."

"What's Ginger supposed to do . . . hold their horses for them while they rob a bank?"

Miss Sadie shook her head. "She's supposed to get married."

With each passing mile, Ginger felt her hope slipping away. She'd escape. No doubt about it, but the way Web and Lane were watching her like a couple of buzzards circling a wounded cub, it wasn't going to be an easy feat. Her best bet was to wait until they were asleep and sneak off then.

Web kept hunching over, and judging from his pale face and trembling hands, Ginger knew the pain in his body was something fierce. She noticed Lane eyeing him from time to time and wondered if he realized the same thing. Maybe she'd misjudged Lane somewhat. He did seem to be keeping a close eye on Web.

Nudging her horse forward, she rode side by side with Lane. "Web's in pain. Maybe we ought to stop for a while."

Lane looked at her askance and frowned. "We ain't stoppin' 'til dark." He glanced at the sky. "That won't be for two more hours."

"But what about Web?"

Lane shrugged. "If he slows us down, we'll get rid of him." He peered closer. "Don't tell me you've suddenly gone and got some daughterly love for the old man."

Ignoring the question, Ginger tried another tactic. "Why push so hard? Do you honestly think anyone's coming after us?"

"I ain't takin' any chances."

Ginger wanted to believe someone would follow. But knowing Blake, he wouldn't spare any more days off the trail. Not for one man's moneybag. But what about Grant? She hadn't allowed herself to think about it. Would he come for her? Did he really think she was worth risking his neck for?

Not that she needed Grant or anyone else saving her. She would be taking care of that herself, as soon as the snoring began from under the tents.

Glowering at Lane, Ginger reined in a little and waited for Web to catch up. "You're feeling pretty rough, huh?"

He nodded, as though speaking would require too much effort. "I tried to get Lane to stop, but he thought we should keep going. You might want to call a stop. You're still the boss around here, aren't you?"

A fierce frown plunged between his eyebrows. "You implying I ain't?"

"I'm not implying anything, but it's pretty clear that Lane thinks he's in charge. And the men are following him, Web."

A cloud of suspicion darkened his eyes as he glanced around the motley group of riders. "Okay, everyone stop right now."

His words, loud and with more authority than she'd heard from him in quite some time, rang in the air and left no doubt that everyone had best do as he said. The fact that his pistol was also drawn reinforced that authority.

Lane pulled his mount to a halt and the rest of the men

followed suit. The subtle act of following the leader wasn't lost on Ginger. Lane reached for his pistol.

"I wouldn't," Ginger said, her voice thick with warning. She might not take the same pleasure in shooting him that she had once thought she might, but she wouldn't let him shoot Web, either.

He slowly moved his hand back to the reins. "What is this?"

"Any of you confused about who leads this outfit?"

Lane's face split into a cajoling smile. "Now, Web. What kinda question is that? Ya know you're the leader around here. Where would we be without Web?" He posed the question to the group. Tension spilled into the air, thick as molasses in winter. "Web, you ain't lookin' so good. You want to stop for a while?"

The challenge in Lane's voice was unmistakable, but apparently Web was in so much pain he didn't notice.

The men watched for any sign of weakness. Ginger spoke up before Web could accept Lane's suggestion. "Web's fine. He's as strong as any of you and can outride and outshoot any of you on a bad day."

Web straightened and threw his shoulders back. "That's right. Anyone doubtin' that?" Finally, he understood what Lane was trying to do. "Now we been ridin' together for a long time. Have I ever let you down?"

No one spoke. As far as outlaw leaders, Web was the best. No one could deny that. This robbery in California would be the first time he'd truly given the men a reason to doubt him. And if he wasn't so close to dying, he probably wouldn't have made that mistake. He would have paid someone to verify the letters.

"That's what I thought," Web said. "Now, let's get movin'."

Web's face clenched suddenly, and his body tensed. He let out a roar of pain just before he lost consciousness and fell from his horse, crashing to the ground.

"Pa!" The word sounded foreign as it flew from Ginger's mouth, but it was the first thing she thought of. She dismounted and ran to him, kneeling next to him. "What's wrong, Web?"

"Looks like I'm not goin' to make it to California, after all."

"It's okay. I'll get you back to the wagon train. Grant will take care of you."

To Ginger's surprise, he nodded. Web might not be the best pa, but he was the only one she had. If there was a chance he might soften up in his last days of life and realize his need for God, then she wasn't going to let the chance slip away.

"Hold on." Lane's boots made short work of the distance between his horse and where Web lay on the ground. "Web's free to go wherever he pleases, but you are comin' with us. We need you to meet that fellow in California. Besides," he sent her a leering grin and his gaze covered her curves. Ginger shuddered. "Did you forget Web's promise?"

"Forget it, Lane. I'm not going to California, and I'm not marrying you."

Before she knew what was happened, her hair felt like he was ripping it from her head as he gripped her braid and yanked her to her feet. He pulled her against him and spoke close to her ear. "You're gonna stop saying that, do you understand?"

"Let her go!" Web's weak voice shot from the ground.

Lane gave him a hard kick that brought tears to Ginger's eyes. "Shut up, old man."

"Lane, you don't have to hurt him. He's been good to you."

"This ain't the way we discussed this," Ames said. He rode forward. "Let go of Ginger. There's no need to hurt her. She'll cooperate without it." His eyes seemed to plead with her not to push the matter.

Surprisingly, Lane listened and unclenched her hair from his fist. She stumbled forward, sending Ames a grateful half-smile.

Ames had a loyalty to her since she'd come to help Miss Sadie nurse the men. She glanced about the group and noted some with hesitance in their eyes. All of the men who had been sick and a couple of the others.

Lane sneered down at Web. "Can you get back in the saddle, old man?"

Ginger knew if he didn't, Lane would leave him to die alone. She knelt next to Web. "I'll help you. If you can't sit alone, you can share my horse and hold on to me."

Web's eyes showed surprise, then a mist appeared. "I'd be obliged."

Ignoring the men, Ginger struggled to help Web to his feet. His bulk nearly knocked her off. "Can you get on the horse after me?"

"I'll try," he gasped.

Ames dismounted and stepped up next to them. "Let me help."

Ginger nodded and climbed onto her horse's back. She held the mount steady while Ames helped Web. He grabbed hold of her as though she was a lifeline, and Ginger realized just how sick Web really was. Would her pa even make it through the night?

Eighteen

Grant rode with Sam Two Feathers and Buddy, who had insisted on joining the two men. "She's my sister," he reminded them. "I'm going even if I have to ride alone." It had been that last threat that had caused the men to relent.

"Look," Sam said. "Someone fell off a horse."

"There's no blood," Grant said. "He wasn't shot."

"Two are riding together."

Grant didn't see that in the tracks, but he knew better than to question Sam about such things and accepted the words as truth.

The outlaws had several hours of travel ahead of Grant and the other two. But with more riders, they were slower. Plus, Sam had agreed to traveling all night, and that had brought them even closer. Following tracks by lamplight tested Sam's skills, but so far, he hadn't disappointed.

"How far ahead do you think they are?"

Sam held up his fingers to his lips and pointed into the woods. Grant's stomach tightened. Were they that close?

Sam placed his hand on his pistol.

"Don't shoot," called a voice from the direction Sam had pointed. "I'm coming out with my hands up."

The stranger rode tall in his saddle, sinewy, with a broad brimmed hat slanted downward across his forehead.

"Hey, Elijah," Buddy called. "What are you doing back here?"

"Good to see you, Buddy," the stranger said.

Grant stiffened at the realization this man rode with the outlaws. Was his gun the one that had shot the fatal bullet into Sarah? "Like Buddy said. What are you doing apart from the outlaw gang?"

"I've been trailing them." He cast a quick glance to Buddy, then back to Grant. "Ginger's in trouble."

"We figured that. Miss Sadie made it back to the camp with Mr. Harrison."

Elijah nodded. "Good. I expected Lane to kill them."

His words sent a cold chill up Grant's spine.

"Lane who? I thought Web was in charge."

"In theory."

The man's demeanor and speech pegged him as an educated man. "What's a fellow like you doin' riding with a bunch of thugs?"

"I have my reasons."

"Thieving and murdering?" Grant heard the bitterness in his voice. For the life of him, he barely contained his anger.

"Do you have a bone to pick with me, stranger?"

The important thing now was to find Ginger and bring her back safely. Confronting the outlaws that killed Sarah could wait.

"No."

"I'm assuming you three are going after Ginger?"

Two Feathers nodded. "We are."

"So am I. May I join you?"

"Can you be trusted?" Grant heard himself saying.

"You should know right now that I'm not part of this outlaw gang." He shot another glance to Buddy. "I might as well go ahead and tell you. I'm here to get you and Ginger away from Web once and for all. Your brother Clem sent me."

"Clem?" Buddy frowned. "That ain't true, Elijah. Clem died when I was just a kid."

Grant decided it was time to remove all the assumption from the air. "No, Buddy. He didn't. I was there. I pulled the bullet out and cleaned the wound."

Elijah nodded. "That's exactly the way Clem told it. What he didn't say is that Lane's the one that shot him. They'd got into an argument about Ginger that day. Clem caught Lane staring at her in the lake. They had a terrible fight, and Clem turned just as Lane shot."

Buddy shook with fury. "I'll kill him."

"No, son," Elijah said gently. "Clem doesn't want that. He's forgiven Lane for what he did."

"Where is he?"

"Clem was sent to prison for his part in the stage robbery. Because a woman died, he was sent up for a long time. Only the fact that his gun hadn't been fired saved him from getting hanged."

"There's more, Buddy." Grant nudged his horse toward the boy. "The woman that was killed was my wife, Sarah."

Buddy stared at him wordlessly, as though robbed of speech. But his eyes reflected his sorrow. He cleared his throat. "All this time, we blamed you for Clem's death, and here you saved him. But we killed your wife."

Buddy's words hit Grant like an anvil. "You blamed me?"

"Ginger said you wouldn't help him and that he died before she left."

Grant gathered a ragged breath. That's why Ginger always seemed to be angry at him. And why lately she'd been playing hot and cold. She was clearly struggling between her feelings for him and her anger that he had allowed her brother to die. "Listen, Buddy. After Ginger ran off, I went to your brother. He wasn't dead—just passed out from blood loss."

"Basically," Elijah said. "The doctor, here, saved your brother's life even though his own wife had just died."

"We have to tell Ginger before she shoots Grant."

Elijah smiled. "I've already told her, but I don't expect she still wants to shoot him, anyway."

Grant's stomach jumped at the implication of the words.

"It will be fully light soon," Sam broke in. "We should move on."

They moved single file. As the sun rose, the sound of gunfire in the distance froze Grant's blood. Without waiting for a reaction from the others, he kicked his mount into a gallop and headed toward the shots, praying he'd find Ginger alive.

Ginger stood, chest heaving, disappointment searing her gut as Lane held her gun and nearly growled as he paced in front of her. She'd only fired off one round when Lane got the jump on her and grabbed her gun. "What did you think you were going to do?" he demanded. "Fight us all?"

She jerked her chin. "If I had to." And she still would, next chance she got. Two things she could bank on: there was no way she was going to let them hurt Web, and she'd take a bullet before she'd marry the likes of Lane Conners. "You aren't touching my pa. You hear me? And you aren't leaving him for the wolves, either. He needs help, and I'm not leaving him."

She didn't see the blow coming, but in a flash, the ground rose up to meet her amid an explosion of pain across her cheek from his fist. "Don't you tell me what you're gonna do, woman. You'll do as I say. I'm the boss here now."

"You're an idiot." A kick to the gut sent her sprawling, gasping for breath.

Ames stepped forward. "Enough, Lane."

"You want what she's getting?"

Ames still hadn't recovered his full strength, so Ginger didn't blame him when he backed down. Lane nodded. "Smart move." A sneer curled his lip, and before anyone knew what to think, he fired point blank. Ames eyes widened, his hand clutched the bleeding wound in his gut. He dropped to his knees and fell face-first, his blood staining the fresh snow that had fallen overnight. Lane eyed the shocked group of men. "Anyone else want to challenge me?"

Apparently no one did.

"You're all a bunch of cowards. Lane's the biggest idiot in the whole camp, and you're going to follow the likes of him?" She braced herself for another blow but dodged just as he reared back to kick her. She grabbed for his foot and sent him sprawling, and her gun dropped to the ground. He roared with rage, but Ginger sprang to her feet and snatched her gun from where he'd dropped it. This time, she kept her back to the woods so she could keep her eye on the whole group. One sweeping glance confirmed that no one was missing. "Now, you listen to me closely. Those so-called letters were nothing more than a scam. If any one of you fools knew how to read your own name, you'd have been able to figure out that Clem wrote them to Elijah. They were trying to get me away from this group when Clem gets out of prison in February."

"It's a lie!" Lane snarled.

"Don't even think about trying to get up, Lane."

She turned toward the group.

"The reason Lane doesn't want to believe Clem is alive is because he's the one that shot him."

"Don't believe her. She's just tryin' to turn you agin' me."

"It's the truth."

Greely stepped forward. "It's true. Lane did it. I seen him with my own two eyes."

Ginger turned to the man. "Then why didn't you ever say anything?"

He shrugged and looked away with shame. "You was so allfired set to blame the doc, it just seemed better to let it go."

"But the doctor saved Clem's life, and all this time . . ." Ginger fought back tears.

"All this time what?" Lane sneered. "You blamed the doc, then you went and got sweet on him."

"That's my business!"

"Ya see? She's lying, and so is Greely."

"No, they aren't."

From the woods, Elijah emerged, pistol brandished, eyes like steel. On the other side of the camp, Grant did the same thing. And Buddy came to her. His eyes grew big when he noticed Web lying unconscious on the ground. "What happened? Did he get shot?"

"No, Buddy. He's sick."

Grant spoke softly. "We'll get him back to camp and try to ease his pain some."

Ginger looked across the camp once more. "Elijah is the one that told me about Clem. I read my brother's letters. No one could have faked them, because he mentioned things that only Clem and I discussed."

"Clem's still alive, huh?" Lane said, his face white.

"Yes, even though you did your best to kill him."

Two Feathers took charge. "Everyone take off your gun belts and give them to Buddy."

As Buddy came to Lane, the man swung around and pointed his pistol, just as a gun went off. Ginger gasped and jumped back. Web's hand shook, but his shot had been true. "He tried to kill my boy," he whispered. Then he lost consciousness once more.

Within a few minutes, all of the men were mounted, their hands tied together and secured to the saddle horns. Sam stood in front of Grant and Ginger. "Grant will escort you two and Web back to the wagon train. They'll likely be at Fort Boise by the time you meet up with them. We'll loop back and meet up with the sheriff back at Fort Hall and then catch up in a few days." He peered close at Ginger. "You'll let Toni know?"

Ginger smiled. "I will. Thank you for coming, Two Feathers."

He nodded. "You were doing pretty well on your own."

"Yeah, but who knows what might have happened once we rode out?"

Without a wagon, Grant constructed a travois to transport Web back to camp. Ginger could barely speak or look at him while they traveled. She simply didn't know what to say. He knew now that Sarah had been killed by Web's gang. And yet he'd been gentle and kind so far in caring for him.

Within a day, they reached the walls of Fort Boise. Just outside the fort, the wagon train had made a temporary camp. Miss Sadie rushed out to meet her. "Oh, thank the Lord."

Barely conscious, Web insisted on speaking to Mr. Harrison before going any further. In moments, the man appeared. He hunkered down next to Web. Slipping beneath the covers, Web pulled out two saddle bags. "This is part of the money. The rest is in the other two saddle bags on Ginger's horse."

Charles's eyes misted. "This will mean a new life for everyone here."

Ginger wasn't too sure what that meant, but she sure was glad to see that money in the right person's hands.

That evening, Blake called a meeting.

"Listen, folks. The snows are too deep for us to make it to Oregon this year." He held up his hands to silence the groans.

"Several of you have come to me with your intention to continue on together. I wish you'd reconsider, but I'm not going to stop you. For those of you who have decided to stay on at the fort for the winter, Mr. Harrison has an announcement and a proposition."

Ginger watched with interest as Mr. Harrison stood on the tailboard of a wagon. "I know we're all getting low on supplies. Many of you have wondered how we can make it through the winter here and still get to Oregon in the spring. God has blessed me, folks. And I'd like to offer each of you the loan of enough for supplies. I intend to start a mercantile when we get settled. You can pay me as crops come in. I am prepared to loan a certain amount, so this will be first come, first served. When I reach the point where my family might suffer, I will not offer any more."

Ginger smiled. This was the way these people would survive. They would rely upon one another and God, and He would bless the land.

She felt a hand on her shoulder and instinctively knew Grant was ready for their talk. Turning, she drew a breath as their gazes locked. He held out his hand and without hesitation, she locked her fingers with his and allowed him to lead her away from the wagons to the river. They stood next to an evergreen tree.

"How do we go forward?" Grant asked, his palm warm against hers.

"However you want, I guess." Ginger swallowed hard.

"You joined the wagon train to kill me?"

Miserably, she nodded and dropped her gaze.

Tucking his finger beneath her chin, Grant raised her head. "You had a lot of chances."

"Yes," she whispered. Why couldn't she breathe?

"Why didn't you do it?"

Ginger knew it was time to stop lying. She didn't want anything between them ever again. "Because I recognized what a good man you were. And . . ."

"And?"

"I fell in love with you almost from the beginning."

His lips twitched. "I remember a lot of choice words from you when I took that arrow out of your leg."

"And you kept your word and never told a soul that I fainted."

"I wanted you to trust me." His gaze never left hers. He unclasped their hands and slipped his arms around her.

Ginger's heart nearly beat out of her chest. "You gave me a crutch."

Nodding, he pulled her closer. "Because I knew you wouldn't want to be stuck without a way to get around."

Lifting her face to his, Ginger's eyes filled with tears. "You saved my brothers' lives. Both of them."

"Because I'm a doctor, and it's what God's given me to do."

Ginger's gaze dropped to his lips. "You do Him proud."

Grant drew a quick breath. "Will you marry me?"

The abrupt question startled Ginger. Her eyebrows rose as she lifted her eyes back to his. "Marry you?"

"I love you."

"But it was my fault Sarah died." Tears spilled over and

flowed down her cheeks. "How can you possibly move on from that?"

"It was not your fault. Sarah was killed by an outlaw's bullet. You were as much an innocent victim as she was."

She could see in his eyes that he believed what he said. Relief flooded her. "Are you sure?" she whispered. With all of her being, she wanted to be this man's wife.

"Does that mean you're saying yes?"

Ginger's mouth curved into a smile. Grant didn't wait for another second, he lowered his head. Ginger had never experienced the new emotions rising inside of her as his warm lips moved over hers. She wrapped her arms around his neck and allowed herself to surrender to his kiss, his touch, his love.

Oregon might be the destination for many of the pioneers, but as far as Ginger was concerned, as long as she remained in Grant's arms, she had reached her promised land.

Epilogue

Three years later, Oregon

The soft strains of "Amazing Grace" filtered softly into the fresh air of a warm summer day in the Willamette Valley as Ginger, Toni, and Fannie walked together from the barn. Ginger loved Sundays, when their friends came and Sam conducted a barn service. It would have to do until the little community had the funds for a real church. For now, Ginger enjoyed watching the children running around the yard and pestering the chickens and working up the dogs into an excited frenzy.

Fannie and Toni each had two children, and Ginger and Grant were well on their way to joining them in numbers. Little Clementine had joined the family nine months after the wedding. And the new baby was due any time.

Sam had been especially long-winded this morning, and by the time he said the final *amen*, the sun beat down on the barn, and everyone was drenched.

"Goodness," Toni said, fanning herself with her hands. "He's going to have to tone it down until this hot spell lets up, or we'll all be cooked before harvest comes."

The three women laughed. Fannie turned to Ginger. "How are you feeling?"

"Hot," Ginger said, grinning. She knew full well what her friend meant.

Nudging her, Fannie urged, "Do you think it'll be this week?"

"I'd be surprised if this baby didn't come before next Sunday."

Truth be told, she'd be surprised if she lasted the night.

"Where do you want these things?" Blake called from the wagon. He held up a basket that Ginger knew from experience would be laden with all sorts of delicious food. Enough to feed an army.

Fannie smiled, blowing a puff of soft red curls from her face. "Set it on the table over there."

"Did you hear we're getting a teacher?" Ginger asked. "That means when our children are old enough, they'll have a real teacher and a real school to attend. Isn't that marvelous?"

"It sure is," Fannie replied, her enthusiasm flashing in her brown eyes. She turned to Toni. "Why are you so quiet all of a sudden? Don't you like the idea of getting a teacher? The township is growing by leaps and bounds."

"I'm thrilled there'll be a teacher for the children. Only . . ." Toni drew a slow breath. "Sam and I won't be here that long."

"What do you mean?" Ginger asked, placing a restraining hand on her friend's arm as she halted her steps and faced Toni. "Where are you going?"

"Oh, Ginger. We can't raise our children here." She swept the air with her hand. "They'll never be accepted by whites. I doubt the school board would even allow half-Indian children to attend school with white children."

"Hogwash. Sammy and Lilith are only a quarter Indian," Ginger said, knowing that didn't matter.

Fannie expelled a soft sigh. "Blake and I have been expecting this. When will you go, and where?"

Brightening, Toni smiled. "We're going to live close to Fort Laramie. The Sioux have a camp close by and come there often to trade. Sam feels a call from God to live close to them and teach them about Jesus. I will also teach the children to read and write." Her voice broke. "I'm honored and grateful that God would choose to use me after all I've done in my past."

Ginger slipped an arm around her friend. "He's given all of us second chances. But I'm going to miss you. And what about our services?"

"Don't worry. We won't leave until after harvest. By then, we hope God will have sent someone to take Sam's place."

"No one could ever take his place. Or yours," Fannie said, sniffing as tears filled her eyes. "But I'm happy that God has led each of us into the life He planned."

"Amen to that," Ginger said. "Now we better get to setting out the food before our children and husbands start complaining."

As if by unspoken agreement, the three women pushed aside thoughts of Toni and Sam's departure and determined to enjoy their day together. Who knew how many Sundays such as this one they had left to share, laugh, and hold onto their dreams of the future?

That evening, while Yuley played his harmonica, Ginger sat lazily on the porch leaning against Grant. They enjoyed a glorious moon and a soft breeze as the sun went down and twilight descended.

Buddy even took a night off from studying for the entrance

exam to medical college back east. If he passed the test, he'd be leaving in a few months to begin his studies. The thought filled Ginger with sorrow, but she knew it was the right thing. And she could no sooner forbid Buddy his chance to live his dream than she could have stopped the rain from falling.

Web hadn't lived to see his first grandchild, but he had lived long enough to make a heart change, and when he died, he saw angels. He would have loved a night like this. But Ginger was happy he would be there to greet them when they reached heaven.

The only other person missing from their lives was Yellow Bird. She had decided to stay on at Fort Boise. She'd fallen in love with an enormous fur trader who loved her to distraction and adored Little Sam.

Two-year-old Clemmie toddled up the steps and plopped herself down on Ginger's legs.

Ginger smoothed her hair and kissed her forehead. "Mercy, child where have you been? You look like a wild animal."

"Unc'a Clem feed chickens. I helped."

"You helped feed the pigs, too, from the smell of things," Miss Sadie grumped from her rocking chair. "I can smell you from here, child. Come on, and let's get you cleaned up."

"Aw, Gwanny."

Miss Sadie glanced at Ginger and shook her head. "The child takes after you."

Ginger grinned. "I'm afraid she does."

"She's perfect," Grant said. "Give your daddy a kiss before you go."

Clemmie landed a fat kiss on his mouth. Watching her daughter cradled in her husband's arms sent waves of joy through Ginger. Her children would grow up under the blessing of God on their lives. Parents, uncles, friends, a good life with God as their center. And her little girl's sweet, if rambunctious, spirit attested to those blessings.

The door closed after them, and Ginger sighed as she settled back against Grant's chest on the wooden porch. "I wonder if a person's heart can get so full it just explodes."

Grant chuckled. "Are you asking for my professional opinion on the matter?"

"I was just thinking about how blessed we are. Friends and family. Miss Sadie is like the mother I never really had." She tried to hide her tears. But it was no use.

Grant wrapped his arms around her tightly. "I love you, you know that?"

"You better, considering . . ." She eyed her big belly, then gave a little gasp. She wouldn't be able to keep her secret much longer.

"You okay?" he asked, pressing a kiss to her hair.

"Just a twinge."

"How many twinges have you been having?"

"Quite a few, to tell you the truth. Relax, Papa." She teased. "This isn't my first baby."

"Ginger, have you been having contractions all day without telling me?"

"Well, I didn't want to miss out on our Sunday, and you would have made me stay in bed all day. This is so much better. Only . . ."

He disentangled from her and helped her to her feet.

Two hours later, Ginger sat up, happily refreshed and much more energetic than she'd been after delivering Clemmie. Another girl had joined their family. "What shall we name your new sister, Clemmie?" Ginger asked her sleepy little girl.

"We keep baby?"

The room erupted into laughter. "You bet we are," Grant said. He lifted Clemmie into his strong arms. "God keeps giving me beautiful, ornery women. I must be the luckiest fellow in the world."

Miss Sadie snorted. "Either that, or you're the dumbest for considering it a blessing."

"Baby name Becky?" Clemmie asked.

"You like that name, honey?" Ginger asked. "Where'd you hear it?"

Clem coughed loudly. "Uh, let's go on out of here and let your ma get her rest."

Ginger grinned at her brother. "Clem Freeman. Do you have a girl?"

"They just came in on the new wagon train."

"You must like her if you're already talking about her."

"My niece has a big mouth, just like her ma."

Again, laughter filled the air. Ginger looked down at her beautiful new daughter. "Sarah."

She lifted her gaze to Grant. His eyes shone with tenderness. "Are you sure?" he asked. She nodded.

Grant knelt down beside her bed. He kissed the baby. Then pressed his lips against Ginger's.

"It's perfect."

Secure in God's love and the love of a large, wonderful family, Ginger closed her eyes as the fatigue overcame her. She drifted to sleep with a smile on her lips.

Dear Reader,

I'm heartbroken to be writing my final reader letter for the Westward Heart series. What a wonderful adventure this has been. I'm truly sorry to see it end and say goodbye to Fannie, Toni, Ginger, and the ensemble cast of characters that made up the wagon train and appeared in each book.

Through Ginger, I chose to end the series with the most difficult of the three heroines to love. I see so much of me in her. Sometimes unlovable, with so much still to learn about His ways and the things that please Him. My prayer is that God will always look at me through eyes of mercy and grace and not punish me according to what I deserve, (Psalm 103:10) lest I be brought to nothing, but to discipline me according His tender mercy.

There was a lot of ugliness, illness, dirt in this book. It unsettled me a little, as my senses were engaged, imagining each scene (my imagination is VERY vivid!). The outlaws in this book were so vile and filthy, because I wanted to contrast for Ginger, the ugliness of sin with the goodness of God revealed in people like Miss Sadie, Mr. Harrison, the sweet innocence of Yuley and Alfie Harrison, and, of course, the heroic and tender grace from a man like Grant. I wanted to show a deep change from where she had come from in her life to the blessed promised land God was preparing for her.

No matter where you are today in your own life, God has a wonderful plan that involves your good. His sweetness makes me smile. His kindness takes my breath away, His love is better than life. He is the ultimate hero. Every beat of my heart is for Him. I pray that as you read this book, God showed you His great desire to pull you from the ugliness of your past. To wipe away the guilt and pain of the past and give you the peace that a child of God must come to as we learn to trust His love and grace.

Ginger asked a question of Miss Sadie, speaking of forgiveness, "If God is God, how can He forget?" Miss Sadie answers with scripture, "He forgets for His sake." God is sovereign, He blots out our past, any confessed sin because He chooses to. It's that simple. Our minds make it so hard to wrap around. But as far as God is concerned, it's a matter of closing a door and never looking back.

And now, as I close the door on this final book in the Westward Hearts series, let me say thank you for taking this journey with me. May God bless you richly as you walk the journey He has set before you, and may He bring you to green pastures, sit you next to still waters, and deepen your roots in Him as He restores your soul.

Tracey Bateman

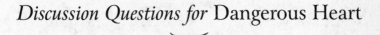

Discussion Questions for Dangerous Heart

1. By the time the book opens, Ginger has been with the wagon train for two months and has come to admire the goodness displayed by the pioneers she's grown close to. If someone like Ginger were to walk into your life, would you be salty enough to make her thirsty for God?

2. Loyalty runs as a thread throughout the book, showing Ginger's true heart beneath the gruff exterior. Who do you know like this? How difficult do you find the task of looking beneath the surface dirt to the cry of the heart?

3. Following up on question number two: What about your own gruff exterior, or the walls you throw up for protection? How deep do people have to look to find your true nature? What will it take, do you think, for God to wipe away all that isn't transparent?

4. As you read *Dangerous Heart*, who did you most identify with, and why? Ginger, the outlaws, Miss Sadie? Or someone else? What do you think your choice says about your self-image?

5. Often Ginger makes wrong choices, knowing there might be consequences she won't enjoy—for instance, being put on water detail when she wants to be free to join the hunters or scouts. God's discipline still offers us a choice. We can either submit and move past the test with confidence, victory, and a new step in our walk with Christ; or we can rebel further and cause more distance between us and God. Do you ever find yourself in the middle of a rebellious choice, having to deal with the consequences of those choices? What do you do when put on the "water detail" of the Lord?

6. When Grant apologizes to Ginger in chapter one, it catches her off guard and chips at her defenses. When was the last time you gave a smile when someone expected you to frown? How does sometimes doing the unexpected tenderize the moment between you and someone you care about? Are you up to a challenge? Give the "soft answer that turns away wrath." Or something equally unexpected to thwart a potentially volatile situation in your life. And if you want, write to me and share the testimony: *author4god@embarqmail.com*.

7. I love the way the people that God has brought into Ginger's life tend to see beyond who she is now to the potential in her, and they tend to speak to that part of her. Grant sees her loyalty; Miss Sadie sees her purity; Blake sees her as a capable scout and gives her chances despite her stubbornness. What does this say about a person "becoming" what people expect—good or bad? Can you give examples of this in entertainment personalities or people you know?

8. Ginger chose to go to the outlaw camp and nurse the men, even though cholera raged. In a parallel, when we become "clean," we often go back to where we came from because we so want our friends to see the new life and want what we have. Was this true in your life? How difficult was it to remain friends with your unsaved friends after you came to Jesus?

9. Ginger believes she can't be with Grant because she feels responsible for his first wife's death. One of the major tools of the enemy of our souls is condemnation. 1 John 3:21 says if our heart doesn't condemn us we have confidence before God. We can know that we belong to Jesus and come before Him with the confidence of a woman who knows she's loved. Do you find yourself believing you aren't worthy of God's goodness? How do you face that lie from the devil?

10. Ginger has trouble believing God can truly forgive someone like Web. She wonders how God can possibly forget, if He's God. Miss Sadie shares scripture with her that God blots out those sins for His own sake. Sometimes it's hard to believe God can forgive someone we can't seem to forgive ourselves. Is there someone in your life you need to forgive, as you realize the very sin you are holding against them is something God has blotted out for His own sake? It can be a process or an instant step. As you pray for God's grace, let Him show you how to walk free of the bitterness of your past.

Tracey Bateman

Tracey Bateman lives in Missouri with her husband and four children. Their rural home provides a wonderful atmosphere for a writer's imagination to grow and produce characters, plots, and settings. In 1994, with three children to raise, she and her husband agreed that she should go to college and earn a degree. In a freshman English class, her love for writing was rekindled and she wrote a short story that she later turned into a book. Her college career was cut short with the news of their fourth baby's impending arrival, but the seeds of hope for a writing career had already taken root. Over the next several years she wrote, hooked up with critique partners, studied the craft of writing, and eventually all the hard work paid off.

She currently has over twenty-five books published in a variety of genres. Tracey believes completely that God has big plans for His kids, and that all things are possible to those who will put their hope and trust in Him.

Visit the author online at traceybatemanbooks.com

Introducing

AVON
INSPIRE

Celebrate the grace and power of Love